Prospects

Edie's devastated. *He's* moved on, and she is stuck in limbo. Will she, *can* she, ever find happiness without him?

Ever since Theo's heart was captured by his wealthy new love Alice, Edie wanders lost and alone. With no money for a debut party and no prospects coming knocking, the bleak title of "spinster" looms ever closer on her horizon.

Edie is determined to find a way to a new life, spinster or not. If she can't have the true love she's lost forever, the very least she can do is become a useful member of society. When Alva Vanderbilt, the richest woman in America, unwittingly comes to Edie's rescue, she's convinced this will be the turning point in her life that plucks her from the depths and delivers her into a full and happy life.

But unexpected events take a shocking turn, plunging Edie's situation into greater depths than ever before. Before she resigns herself to genteel poverty and a loveless state, is there really no way forward for her? Or is destiny about to lend a hand?

Perhaps I Will

EDIE IN LOVE
BOOK 2

JANE SUSANN MACCARTER

Copyright © 2021 by Jane Susann MacCarter

Publishing Services provided by Paper Raven Books
Printed in the United States of America
First Printing, 2021

Jane Susann MacCarter
Perhaps I Will
Edie in Love Series
Book Two

Hardcover ISBN= 978-1-7368789-1-0
Paperback ISBN= 978-1-7368789-3-4

Subjects: Edith Kermit Carow, Theodore Roosevelt II, Alice Hathaway Lee, United States First Lady, 26th President of United States, Gilded Age, Victorian romance, 1880s politics, coming-of-age

To my dear daughter, Mindy MacCarter Mangel, ever my cheerleader who holds my life's compass in her hand and also in her heart.

Perhaps I Will

Only slang can describe it best: In the spring of 1879, I was well and truly "sockdologized."

That is, well and truly "flattened by fate" at the hand of Theodore Roosevelt himself. (Metaphorically speaking, of course...)

In those long-ago days, sockdologize meant "to deliver an unexpected, powerful, and sickening punch to the gut."

Although nobody uses this slang anymore, that word loomed large in our lives back then after Abraham Lincoln's assassination. Just as Lincoln was laughing at a comic line in Our American Cousin, the last play he ever saw— "You sockdologizing old man-trap!"—he was blown into eternity by an assassin's bullet.

Although my "sockdologizing" was not physical, still it flattened me, both personally and spiritually. When Theo cast me aside in favor of Alice, my "spotless Edie" persona vanished forever, and a wary spinster took her place.

Tuesday

15 April 1879

Finally ... I achieve a major, happy "tidal wave" (amid the stagnant gray pond that comprises most of my life). I win a literary competition sponsored by the *New York World* newspaper with a detailed essay on "Secular Humanism Versus Christian Values in Contemporary New York City Society." There is no tangible prize nor money—just glory and (yes) pride, plus my name in the paper.

But yes, I *am* proud. I've finally accomplished something that makes *both* my parents proud of me at the same time, together.

A few days later, here I am back at the Roosevelt house again after school; Conie and I sit at their back parlor table as we labor over homework while Bamie reads us the latest missive from Theo.

"Say, Edie, Teedie mentions you specifically here. He says, 'Will you please congratulate Edith for me about winning the *New York World's* literary competition?' ... And so, consider yourself now congratulated by Brother in person."

Both sisters chuckle indulgently, and I smile too … although I keep looking at Bamie's chubby hands holding the letter. I want to glimpse T's own, dear, familiar handwriting against the unfamiliar stationery.

Then I see the embossed black lettering at the top of each sheet of stationery: it's emblazoned with the words *CHESTNUT HILL, Brookline, Massachusetts.*

Theo wrote this letter while visiting Alice at her family's estate at Chestnut Hill, just six miles from Harvard.

Life is *never* going to return to the way I so often dreamed it would. I've been "sockdologized," and so my dream life goes on now without me.

Life is flowing into a strange, new, difficult stretch of the river. *I* must make my way as best I can.

SUNDAY

11 May 1879

Yesterday, according to the *Times*, two railroads—the Central Pacific and the Union Pacific—literally, physically met in the middle of the American West at Promontory Point, Utah. There, a golden spike was pounded in, joining the two sets of rails and two competing railroads together. Such fanfare! It's so exciting even to think about it. How *fast* everything seems now in these modern days! Dear Lord, what glorious fun it would be for Theo and I to ride the rails for a thousand miles or more ... Dream on ...

FRIDAY

23 May 1879

Just like he did two years ago—same time of year, same place—Theo once again will host the leisurely, extended annual Harvard visit for the special people in his life.

But this year, *I* am not one of them.

I'm sure it's because of Alice.

T now loves *her* better—more deeply, richly, and passionately—than he ever did me. I can just tell without even properly meeting her yet.

How abashed and slightly embarrassed he must be by what he considers our childish "puppy love"—even though it's *my* alpha and omega and always will be.

T's Cambridge invitation list includes Conie and Bamie (of course), Elliott (home again now from a term at boarding school), Aunt Annie, and Miss Mittie. He's looking forward to them spending a few days in Cambridge (and I quote here from T's last letter to his family) so they can "meet the best of the belles of Boston."

His letter continues: "They are a very sweet set of girls, and I really know them far better than I do most of my former NY friends. I already know Alice much better than I do *any* NYC girl."

There! Yet *another* twist of the knife.

I'm idiotic to even *want* to keep hearing Theo's letters. If I had a sensible brain, I'd make an excuse to leave the premises. Or I should paste that good, old, trusty Mona Lisa smile back on my face and tell the Roosevelt sisters, "How glad you must be that Teedie has so many new friends!" Then, I can (as unobtrusively as possible) change the subject.

But I don't. I *can't*. Theo's letters are a drug to me, even as laudanum is for poor Papa. Even as Theo's news pierces my heart, I simply *must* know what he is doing now … where he's going, who he's seeing … and what he's planning to do next.

Enough—now it's too much to even bear thinking about.

Saturday

7 June 1879

I can scarcely believe it: my school days are *over*.

All my many years at Miss Comstock's—with the attendant dramas, hopes, fears, joys, and sorrows—are done and gone, just like that. *Poof!*

I find myself graduating second in my class of 1879—twenty-seven girls, coming in immediately after Fanny Smith (*of* course ... wouldn't you just know it—at the head of her class and with an engagement ring, too!).

Conie comes in at number seven, which is still respectable, and her family in attendance is very pleased.

Theo isn't there.

In the Great Room, Miss Comstock herself hands out diplomas as we each move toward the front of the line when our name is called. She looks right through me with her handsome, piercing black eyes—I know suddenly I'm going to miss her keenly. Too bad about that now. Time is rushing by too quickly to even draw breath. I can scarcely take in the enormity of it all.

At the reception afterward, most of the graduating girls are trilling at one another with cascading giggles and copious tears. So many are already engaged … fluttering their left hands to show off much-sought-after engagement rings.

Unlike the other girls, I don't cry or giggle. I *do* keep smiling—so serene am I. I've always done "serene" *very* well. When girls come to hug me, I hug them back. But I'm still in a sort of trance. Where to next?

In just two months—on my eighteenth birthday—I'll officially become a young woman. A mysterious, challenging new role awaits me, ready or not.

My family—Mamma, Papa, Em, and even Mame and Grandfather Tyler (because he paid my tuition for all of these years)—all attended the ceremony and rejoice with me.

Many Roosevelts are there, too, cheering Conie on—Miss Mittie, Aunt Annie, Bamie, and Elliott. Theo, though, is "still too busy" finishing up spring term and "unable to attend."

Most class of 1879 Comstock graduates are already planning their coming-out parties; most opt for this September or October, which bring less oppressive heat and better weather for dancing.

Conie keeps begging off having a coming-out party, trying to delay the inevitable as long as possible.

I know Conie deeply fears and dreads this unfortunately compulsory aspect of growing up female and growing up rich. She also dreads anything to do with … how shall I say … the Great Mystery—the personal aspects of life with a husband.

I, *too*, pretend to beg off. With a smile and a blithe shrug, I deflect questions like "And when will *your* coming-out party be, Edith?" (which is a mighty mean thing to ask me because it's generally known that my prospects to make an excellent match are "minimally modest" to put it politely.)

How did I arrive at adulthood so fast?

I used to *long* to be grown-up and autonomous, but that was when I thought I was going to be with Theo.

Adulthood is mysterious and scary now without Theo by my side.

I wish I could wait until twenty-one to be considered an official adult, the way men do. But, worse luck, that's just the way society determined things to be—women at eighteen and men at twenty-one.

In less than two months, *I* will turn eighteen. So will Alice Hathaway Lee. And I know which one of us faces the future with anticipation and a smile.

Friday

20 June 1879

A bracing new breeze now blows through the charitable organizations of New York City. I aim to hitch my efforts at "good deed doing" to the tail of this benevolent gale in September, once I return from summer visits to the relatives.

It's all about the birth of a new movement called COS—the Charity Organization Society.

Perhaps I Will

I heard all about it from Mrs. Josephine Shaw Lowell, a striking, dark-eyed young widow with fiery passion in her heart and belly. She spoke recently at the Fifth Avenue Presbyterian Church, updating the special report she presented to the New York State Board of Charities. She says that COS aims to bring together the "scientific method and good sense"—as well as more compassion—to existing charitable efforts to help the "poor and wretched of this fair city."

Yes, I've *always* been aware that life was—and still is—wretched for tens of thousands of New Yorkers. My "poverty" could be compared to "great wealth" to a lot of people in this vast city. But I had no clear idea of just how *unspeakable,* how untenable, this wretchedness could really be … real, grinding, starving poverty—especially after five *years* of financial depression, which newspapers tell us reached fourteen percent unemployment among breadwinners.

I took copious notes at her lecture. Mrs. Lowell used phrases like, "We must use a scientific approach," "We must investigate, register, and supervise all applicants for charity," "It is imperative to identify and coordinate the resources and activities of applicable private philanthropies," and "We aim to establish centralized clearinghouses to collect information about the individuals and families receiving assistance."

Just *why* must such things be changed? Isn't "doing good deeds"—in and of themselves—reason enough?

Not for Mrs. Lowell, who explains, "We must work to ameliorate the *massive suffering caused by destitution* and the growth of poverty and vagrancy in urban areas. We must reduce conflict between the classes by employing a rational system of scientific charitable administration."

Hmm … yes … "Reduce conflict between the classes."

I can definitely relate to that.

There are numerous class and society levels in this city, with many permutations. Although the Roosevelt's fine old name and Knickerbocker heritage—together with my family's genteel lineage of Kermits, Tylers, and Carows—are considered of equal stature among members of New York high society, it's a fact that the size of our own family purse and the renown of our respective *pater familia* are as different as night and day.

This is what puts me on a different rung, miles lower than Theo's enviable, lofty status.

Although I'm grateful for my modest blessings and I thank God daily for a house to live in, my own narrow bed, and simple food on the table, I *know* I could just as easily have been born to one of the nameless, faceless thousands who go to bed hungry every night.

At the conclusion of her talk, Mrs. Lowell urged that "existing charities will eventually be changed into coordinated private agencies, so that greater social harmony will result from the mutual respect that *will* eventually develop, as volunteers … *(like me)* … and staff will experience greater contact and relationships with poor families seeking assistance."

Yes, this is a noble calling. I aim to be a part of it.

But for now…

Just now, I find myself giving in to weakness, self-pity, and inertia because, well, truth be told, I'm already *tired* of doing good deeds. (And I've barely gotten started.)

I need a change of scene. I'm so tired of thinking about poor people, of whom even Our Lord said, "For ye have the poor with you always, but Me ye have not always."

I need Theo. Or maybe I need a vacation. I'm truly thankful I shall have one again this summer. Theo or no Theo, at *least* I shall swim in the ocean again. I'll braid daisy-chains and pick wildflowers. I'll sit on the shaded Tyler veranda and drink sweet tea. I'll spend time with Grandfather Tyler and my Kermit relatives and surreptitiously explore the possibility of any of them possibly helping to subsidize my launch into society. Because Theo's love so obviously now belongs to another, I must make another life for myself—one quite different from what I'd planned years ago. I must soon "test the waters" and start creating possibilities of a life without Theo, which can *only* be one of two things: a life where I am married to someone else, or … life as an independent spinster of very modest means who does good for others and lives a life of circumspect gentility.

Don't even ask. No other choices exist for me. As I've said before, Mamma would faint dead away should I ever consider "working in trade" as a shopkeeper or lady in a flower shop.

I know that a coming-out party—horribly expensive as they are—would introduce me to a whole new crop of eligible young men. (Yes, invitations can be, and are, sent far and wide to likely families and candidates, even those we may not yet personally know.)

Yes, I *know* that America's current economy is (to quote the newspapers) "shaky and uncertain." I *know* Papa can't afford to give me a coming-out party on his own, even under the best of times—and right now is hardly that. I am *still* quietly hurt and mutely surprised that no other relative has come forward to help us out. Grandfather Tyler loves me dearly. I *know* he does. His financial situation is very, very comfortable, although he is careful and almost never spends money on what he considers to be "frivolous or superfluous" things.

But I suspect he has *no* idea of how flat and slim is our family purse. I doubt he knows nor cares that my gowns are three and four years old now—and getting older all the time, despite Mame gamely trying her best to update them with different laces, ruffles, buttons, and inset panels.

Not to sound too mercenary or avaricious—and I suppose I truly *am* mercenary to even *think* about it—*but…*

I *know* my Tyler and Kermit relatives could all readily afford to fund the cost of a coming-out party for me. So why don't they step forward and do so? Is something wrong with me? Is there some quality *missing* in me? Does Grandfather

Tyler consider me and my future prospects frivolous, too?

I am too proud to beg, of course—and so are Mamma and Papa (I'm not sure about Em or Mame, though, if given the chance). So here I am … here *we* are, going blithely through the days, as time continues to tick, tick, tick away the minutes and the hours as they become weeks, and months, and years.

I'd best continue as I've started out—doing good deeds on behalf of the poor. It's almost impossible to go wrong by being truly benevolent, be it in Heaven or on Earth.

And meanwhile (as well you may ask!), what has Theo been doing all this time?

Fretting about "Sunshine," of course.

Did I tell you before? I don't think I wrote it in this journal earlier, so I'll tell you now: Alice's family's pet name for her is Sunshine. Theo adores that name for her, too.

All I can do in response to this knowledge is emit a deep, long sigh.

Sunshine.

Lordy, Lordy...

Wouldn't you just know. Yes, I've already gleaned some between-the-lines nuggets of information about Alice Lee from various friends and folks: she's an average student in school; bored with natural science, far preferring to play tennis, go dancing, and attend parties instead of reading classical novels; bored by poetry; and she detests anything to do with ancient philosophies. Even so, with such shortcomings, Alice is *so* beautiful and *still* represents the heart and soul of sunshine—in the best sense of the word—to everyone she knows.

Here I am, selfishly hoping that the true Alice within is both shallow, thoughtless, callow, and maybe even cruel—but she's not, at *all.*

Everyone loves Alice (whether she's shallow or not). Girls, fellows, and family love her unconditionally. She's the Sunshine of their lives.

Even now, after more than sixty years, I can still feel the desolation when I compare myself to Alice. I weigh myself in the warmth of her sunshine and still come up wanting.

———◆———

Conie still reads me her brother's letters from school. (And, like the pathetic, whimpering idiot that I am, I still listen with rapt attention.) Because Theo *dreads* being apart from Alice for most of the summer, Conie tells me, he's invited the entire family (both Lees and Roosevelts) to come up to Harvard for Class Day before the term ends.

I'll put it in words that Conie used to describe to me just how it all came about: "After the Harvard Class Day ceremonies, Theo escorted Alice to not one but *two* parties, one right after another! And later, in the twilight, Theo and Sunshine sat together, watching the sway of tinted Chinese lanterns that hung in the Yard, listening to songs by the Harvard Glee Club. At ten o'clock, the songs ended, and as the rest of us trundled off to our hotel beds, Theo and Alice walked over to Memorial Hall and danced until midnight. The band even played 'Alouette,' which everyone sang along with, of course. I adore that song! I mean, who wouldn't? Then the dance concluded with a rollicking version of 'O Dem Golden Slippers.' Oh, I'd have liked to have seen Teedie dance to that! I'll bet he looked just like a grasshopper."

I merely smile back at Conie and nod, with what I *hope* looks like serenity and probity. (But my cheeks hurt from smiling, and the frost-covered boulder in my gut must be endured indefinitely.)

At this point, I simply have no words, outside of the running commentary inside my head.

Monday

30 June 1879

Here's a surprising turn of events. My spinster Aunt Kermit—my great-aunt on Papa's side—died suddenly yesterday at her summer place in Oceanic, New Jersey.

Her brother, Earl, telegraphed the news to us. She went to bed feeling poorly and just never woke up.

I can scarcely believe she's gone. I somehow thought she'd be there forever. Although she was "distant" and always a bit strict with me, I know ... I *know* ... she wanted only the best for me and the women of my family. She *was* seventy-five with a perpetually "fluttering" heart—a heart that will flutter no longer.

A heart condition that I live with right now at age 87, far older than "just" 75.

Most anything can happen to someone beyond the "three score and ten years" that the Bible decrees to be the proper amount of "days of our years."

In idle curiosity last night, I looked up the verse in the Book of Psalms, chapter 90, verse

10: "The days of our years are threescore years and ten; and if by reason of strength they be fourscore years, yet is their strength, labor, and sorrow; for it is soon cut off, and we fly away."

Strength. Labor. Sorrow. And then we fly away...

I wonder if Great Aunt Kermit had to labor much in her life—I'm guessing probably not. At least not literally.

But did she know sorrow? She must have. She had no husband, no children, and no immediate family to call her own (except for her beloved brother, Earl, of course). That's probably why she was so generous to the family of her loving but unreliable nephew, my Papa, Charles Carow. Aunt Kermit's prim and proper evenings—endlessly knitting and tatting, while her brother read her tidbits from the newspaper—must have held much suppressed, unvoiced desolation.

And strength? Of course, she had it. She had a great plenty as a spinster creating for herself a quiet yet noble and upright life and helping her nephew's family with "subsidized rents" in various Manhattan dwellings. (So we didn't end up on the street.) Now, from the great beyond, Great Aunt Kermit helps us still. Although bachelor brother Earl is her chief heir, he respected her wishes to remain private about certain matters (i.e., my father) by giving our family two bequests, ostensibly out of his own portion of inheritance.

One bequest is the old lady's writing desk to me, her great niece. Both she and Mamma knew and approved of my studies and my own personal writings—heaps of poetry and essays.

But the second bequest is going to change our family dynamic beyond our wildest dreams. Through Earl, we Carows are finally going to receive a sum of *money.*

It's enough to put down a cash deposit—finally!—on a house of our very own.

Yes, there *will* be a moderate-sized mortgage on the new house, which is a deep concern to me. Nobody *I* know has a mortgage—so shameful and dangerous they are—but still, needs must. However, I'm thankful there *is* such a thing as a mortgage to help us purchase our own house. No more being "meekly grateful" for subsidized rent and no more living in a house that is not our own.

Wonderful news, *yes*. Sort of.

Because ... although the bequest was a deeply kind gesture, the dollar amount itself was modest. And the thing is, Great Aunt Kermit's death means literally that we *have* to move—our rented house is being sold out from under us to settle her estate.

I heard Mamma and Papa talking about it last night—and Mamma and Papa talked to me about it today because it affects my future as much as it does theirs. (And I *am* their financial advisor, after all.)

In short, there will be *no* money for any coming-out party—modest or otherwise. Acquiring a house of our own is far more important and momentous than any silly debut party—even if it means I will probably be a spinster for the rest of my life.

Perhaps I Will

WEDNESDAY

9 JULY 1879

Sometimes life changes with breakneck speed. At this time one month ago, we lived as "subsidized renters" in one of Great Aunt Kermit's several "income houses" in the city.

Now, just one month later, we're moving into a small but still smart brownstone at 114 East 36th Street in Manhattan, the first house that we've ever owned, all by ourselves (us and the bank together, that is). Our new neighborhood is respectable (well, mostly, I'm fairly sure), if not exactly "desirable." Either way, it is "respectable *enough*" for us Carows and, finally, a place to truly call our own. All I can say is … God bless you, Aunt Kermit! Our new parlor is surprisingly large, which pleases Mamma to no end because it easily holds all of our front-room furniture, which came into the family at the time of her marriage to Papa.

The real estate agent, a good friend of Grandfather Tyler's eldest grandson, is efficient, effective, and more than a little flirty with me. He has a very annoying way of inserting the words "at this point in time" into most every sentence. I do not flirt back.

It still seems unreal to me that Miss Comstock's School is a closed book for me now. I am done with girlish things now, especially because I'm becoming an official marriageable young lady.

No more school … no more close proximity to the Roosevelt mansion (physically, socially, or emotionally) … no more familiar old rental house … no more future life with Theo.

I'm on my own now, *that's* for sure, with no turning back.

Wednesday

6 August 1879

Today, the day of my eighteenth birthday, dawns hot and glorious. Thus far, it's also achingly lonely.

I actually pull the sheet over my head for a few minutes, burrow into my pillow, and try not to think.

But I can't *help* thinking.

No trip to Tranquillity for me this year. Who knows? Possibly (probably) never, ever again.

Yes, our family visited Grandfather Tyler's seaside place this summer. But what does it matter? Whether I'm home or by the sea, Theo is now "cleaved" to another.

Finally, I untangle the sheet from my face— I'm also impatient and angry at the world— pivot my bare feet around toward the floor, and stand up.

I am stern with myself: "*No sniveling. Think of the worthy Mrs. Lowell, the inspiring woman reforming Manhattan's charity systems—now, she wouldn't snivel.*"

A hidden core of me silently retorts, "Of *course* she wouldn't snivel. She *is* called 'Mrs.' Lowell for a reason, even if she's now a widow. At one time, she was both wanted and wed."

I vow, like a prayer, to redouble my efforts. I'll read twice as many improving books this summer and work twice as hard at helping the less fortunate ... so I won't have time to *think* too much.

Thursday

7 August 1879

And so I've begun. There's less sighing and pining, more industry and probity, and no more thinking too much, which is bound to lead me to madness, sooner or later.

Here's a list of new books I aim to finish before the autumn solstice rolls around:

Swinburne's *Life of Blake*

Gilmore's *Life of Coleridge*

Brown's *Life of Southey*

Henry James' *Watch and Ward*

Thackeray's *Pendennis*

... plus I shall re-read two of Dickens' novels: *Great Expectations* and *A Tale of Two Cities*.

I'll be tackling Swinburne first. (Oh, joy.)

LATER this evening:
I must make an admission, though it shames me to do so.

I can't help watching the mail for a letter from Grandfather Tyler—from somebody, *anybody* among my discreetly affluent relatives—announcing the surprise gift of a debut party for me.

While certainly neither vast nor widely known, Grandfather Tyler's financial reserves are considered "very comfortable" and more assuredly ample.

I'm being selfish here, I *know* that, but still...

Theo is out of reach to me now, most likely forever. He's in love with someone else. And that is that—a truth that doesn't bear closer examination.

I ask myself honestly: could *I* ever fall in love with someone else? Someone who isn't Theo?

I *think* that the answer is ... *no.* My heart tells me that I'll never love another man in the way that I love him.

But could I *marry* someone else, nonetheless?

Make a new, married life with another man? One whom I might respect and like, even if I don't truly love him?

Could I co-create children with someone like this—children who are not also Theo's?

Am I willing—and able—to make a home with such a man? A home of our own, a life of our own?

A wave of revulsion washes over me then, followed by an ache of desolation.

But my answer to this situation is ... *perhaps.*

It's either a strange, deflated half-life with someone else ... or a spare, spinster life with little money, doing good works, knitting, and keeping cats.

Make a choice. Take your pick. No other path forward is possible.

Friday

8 August 1879

I've been mulling over *why* Grandfather Tyler doesn't help me with a coming-out party. Here's what I think: Grandfather seems to love me best when I'm behaving like a sweet and studious little girl—someone *chaste and innocent* who lives only for her books and doing charitable deeds for others. Like Aunt Kermit.

He loves someone who never dreams of anything … else … like the Great Mystery of marriage.

Grandfather wants to keep me pliable and child-like indefinitely—and never allow me to grow up. He especially dreads the possibility of me making an unwise marriage, as did Mamma (although she had no other offers at the time, or so Mame told me once).

Oh yes—one more thing: I finally received an eighteenth birthday gift from Theo today, shipped (I see by the postmark) from Brookline, Massachusetts, home of the inimitable Alice.

It's a book. It's what fashionable ladies call a "gift book"—elegant enough to reside indefinitely on a marble-topped parlor table. The book is titled *Lucile*, a well-received "story poem" by the excellent Owen Meredith.

It's inscribed in Theo's unmistakable handwriting: "To Edith K. Carow on her 18th birthday from her sincere friend Theodore Roosevelt."

Sincere Friend.

Sincere Friend.

No words can express how beaten and bruised I feel just now.

My "sincere friend" has well and truly beaten me with a hickory stick without knowing it ever happened.

Friday

15 August 1879

Theo's results arrived from Harvard yesterday. (I have this on good authority from Conie and Bamie in the former's weekly letter to me.)

He received superb grades. (Of course.)

Another note: to keep Alice interested in him (because she makes no secret of her abhorrence of "science and bugs"), Theo announced he's "going into politics" instead.

No more will he dream nobly of becoming a naturalist or natural historian. As Conie wrote in explanation, "He's going into politics on behalf of the public welfare. To do some *good* … kind of like what you're doing—only in a different way."

Saturday

16 August 1879

Theo is spending much of his summer vacation in Oyster Bay at Tranquillity.

I wasn't invited this year. (Nor ever will be again, I suppose.)

I'm not surprised.

(Desolate, yes, and unutterably tired, at times ... but surprised? No.)

Now, in mid-August—during the time when I used to visit Theo at Tranquillity—Theo has instead gone to Chestnut Hill and will continue on to Maine afterward.

Conie writes that Theo vows "not to return until he's tough as a pine knot."

If that's his aim, I'm sure he will hit the mark most ably.

It's unbearable in the city just now. Oppressively humid air makes even breathing a chore. The smell of rapidly accumulating, uncollected garbage in the street makes me want to vomit.

But still, I press on through the days. What else can I do? Many days, I perform my good deeds while clenching my teeth. Lately I've been "darkening the door"—all right, trying to make myself *useful*—at the New York Children's

Perhaps I Will

Orthopedic Hospital, a place of *so* many good intentions, if fewer actual cures, which was founded by dear Greatheart himself. There, I read stories to sick (or dying) children and pat the hands of frightened (or grieving) parents.

Sorry about what I just said about "clenching my teeth"—they *are* "interesting days" but I'd much rather be off with Theo somewhere, slogging through muddy bogs like we used to and collecting obscure specimens of *Odonata* (dragonflies). But even Theo can no longer do that. He hasn't the time—there's that Harvard degree to complete first and then a new career to materialize to provide a means to a living with Sunshine in his life. There's no time for bug collecting these days … *Dear Lord*, how I keenly miss the beauty of those long-ago shared days with him…

Staying home and sulking does me no good, either—I tried that method last Tuesday and felt even worse. It's too hot for dances or supper parties—I don't get invited to many of those anymore. Everyone seems to be paired off anyway.

No doubt I'm growing too boring. *And* too old. I'm no longer a sweet, young thing. After all, I'm eighteen now, getting along in age but not yet engaged, thus eminently "suspect."

And you know how young men are these days … chasing silly sixteen-year-olds.

Monday

25 August 1879

More news to report from the Roosevelt sisters: giddy with positive gossip, they write that "Alice is much kinder to Theo now!" Theo, in turn, writes to his family that "I feel like I'm 'coming home' whenever I go to Alice's house now at Chestnut Hill."

With good-natured consternation, Bamie also writes that Theo and Elliott—"Nell"—have fallen into a summer pattern of "challenging each other with physical contests—and I don't think it's altogether for their mutual good, either!"

Be it rowing, swimming, sailing, or shooting, Theo and Nell duke it out head-to-head, hand-to-hand. Nell generally comes out the worse for wear.

Poor, dear boy! Even one so blinded by Theo as *I* am readily admits that, right now, Elliot is *far* better looking, more charming, and attractive than Theo on even one of his best days. But all of us girls worry that Nell drinks far too much. For the time being, though, we say nothing. We hope he may yet grow out of it.

Nell's tendency toward suffering mysterious seizures has seemingly abated. He's now a young banker in Manhattan society—even though he secretly hates banking. (After all, the fellow must do *something*, and banking is as good as anything—and well thought of by high society.)

Bless his soft, all-too-agreeable heart!

Friends of both sexes *flock* to him, probably because Nell has all of Bamie's class and poise with none of her severity. Also, just like Conie, Elliott has a strong tendency to "gush," but his warmth is actually more genuine than hers.

(Truth be told, Conie seems a little lost these days. Low in her mind—I must ask her about it soon if she doesn't snap out of it.)

"Our Nell" remains adorable, open, decent, and generous, but … there's just no *substance* to him like there is in Theo.

Nell only seems happy—in a wistful, nay somber, sort of way—when intent upon "finding some fun and mischief."

But grown-up life isn't all about having fun. I worry, more and more each day, about the dangerous path Nell follows. Where can it ultimately lead?

Wednesday

27 August 1879

I'm stumbling on the piano—over and over as I make myself practice last year's popular song "In the Evening by the Moonlight"—when the postman jangles our doorbell and slips a letter through the mail slot into the entry hall.

I stop my music on a discordant note. For a rare moment, I am alone in the house.

I move with speed to discover what the postman might have left for us … no, left for *me*.

In addition to what looks like two bills, there's a letter from Conie, writing from Tranquillity.

Heedless with worry—and excitement—I rip open her letter and pour over its brief contents.

Conie has met a man.

That kind of man.

An eligible man.

Scanning the letter hurriedly, I read that she's met him through Elliott. The man in question was Nell's guest at Tranquillity for several days.

She met an *eligible* man, just like that.

Conie goes on to describe him: Doug Robinson, a Scots-American born to a distinguished family, also a graduate of Oxford University in England.

He's six years older than she is, and he's plainly smitten with her. There's more: she writes that she doesn't feel a *thing* for him.

Nothing. Not even a particle.

He's rich, though. That must certainly count for something. Miss Mittie must be thrilled to the skies. The Roosevelt funds are *not* what they once were while Greatheart still lived.

Conie writes that Doug is "well on his way to making a sizable fortune in real estate, here in the USA, where he's lived for a few years."

I read between the lines here…

It sounds to me as if Conie hasn't decided whether to pursue things further, although her mother seems *definitely* to be urging action.

Conie writes, "Douglas … Doug … is a big man—tall, plain, and seemingly gruff. However, he has a tender heart, and he says he truly loves me, since the first day he met me. But I do *not* love *him*, and I don't think I ever will. I don't think I ever *can*. And therein lies the problem. I find myself crying, worrying, and wondering, with no let-up in sight."

Oh Dear God, *this* will never do … poor, hapless Conie.

My life changes during the time it takes for me to read Conie's letter.

Here I am … out of school, now an official young woman, doing those *interminable*, often infuriating good deeds, when what I *really* want to do is be with darling Teedie, read books, roam around in nature, and retreat from the world. (Fat chance of that now.)

And somehow, here is Conie, actually attracting an eligible man who—no doubt ... *no doubt*—will soon be asking her to marry him. She would be thrilled to the *skies* if Doug were her "right man," but even if he isn't, shouldn't she still be content and reconciled to make a good bargain with life?

I would if I was Conie. Wouldn't I? Or perhaps I'd be just as desolate. Or something even worse.

Thursday

28 August 1879

Conie's latest letter to me, which arrived today while I was teaching some young Slovenian girls to make buttonholes at the Young Woman's Christian Association, is a happiness-damper for me in every way.

Oh, why do I even *read* her letters, especially the ones written from Tranquillity? Especially if doing so always makes me so sad? Why do I even write *back* to Conie, when I know that her replies to the same will make me sadder still?

Furious with myself, I *make* myself set up a new still life to paint, splurging on a new canvas and some fresh oil paints. I *try* to imagine myself as Rosa Bonheur the Second, painting animals—animals are her specialty—and people and landscapes with luscious colors. I still write reams of poetry (some of it is even quite good), heaps of essays (but no more romance stories—they're still far too painful.) But my heart isn't in any of it. What's *wrong* with me? Why, *why* can't I move on with my life?

Conie also wrote me that, "for two days and nights, Teedie has been spending time with Alice and her family at Chestnut Hill en route to another of his strenuous trips to Maine."

Conie then related how Alice went with Theo to a beach party, walked with him through the woods, showed off her skills at tennis, and served as his flirtatious partner at a barn dance. Conie concluded by saying, "Alice is sweet and friendly but seems also to be of two minds—and she makes *no* commitments or promises to Teedie, poor boy!"

With no guarantees, Theo continued on north to Maine. *I* finally set up a still life assemblage in the brightest corner of my bedroom: a Waterford crystal vase full of dried purple statice flowers, an old pair of my gloves crumpled artfully around the base, and a folded theater program (like a miniature paper tent) behind the vase. It looks off-center somehow. Like me...

Wednesday

10 September 1879

I never heard what happened to Theo in Maine, but Conie *did* gush to me—in person this time because she's home from Tranquillity for the season—"Guess what! Teedie's bought a two-wheeled tilbury for calling on Alice."

A "dog cart," they call it these days. I am told his trusty horse, Lightfoot, easily pulls it at a smart trot without even breathing hard.

Conie raves about the charming "lamps" on the fashionable vehicle and its gleaming lacquer work. Pike's Stable in Cambridge has done a top-notch job!

I'm told that the seat on a dog cart is just barely big enough for two slim individuals. The man's right thigh will definitely touch the girl's left thigh (imagine, touching thighs!) on such a rig as this. Yes, there will also be a lap rug, just big enough to wrap around the two pairs of "companionable" legs. (Mamma always says I should say *limbs*, not *legs*. She says it's vulgar to say *legs*. I hope she never finds this journal to learn just some of the shocking things I *do* talk about —a lot worse than legs versus limbs.)

Sounds like Theo bought it as a twenty-first birthday present for himself. After all, in another month, he'll reach the age of majority. Or is it maturity? I must look that up.

I still don't like my still life set-up, so I've started a series of charcoal drawings, sketchings from life: Papa reading a newspaper, Mamma making miles of tatting, Em agonizing over a book of conversational French, and Mame gazing out the window (and possibly yearning for the home of her youth in Scotland).

My skills are ... decent. But they're *not* genius ... and I'd hardly even say they're *good*. They're merely therapy for a broken heart.

Conie says Theo immediately went rolling in his "dog cart" all the way down Mount Auburn Street in Cambridge, heading toward Chestnut Hill. Conie adds, with an arch lift of her left eyebrow, "Do you know what the neighbors call him now? He told me so himself in a note, and he only thought it funny. It didn't bother him a bit—they call him 'that swell in the dog cart!'"

The rest of Conie's visit is filled with far more somber reports: Doug Robinson continues to pursue my friend relentlessly, although she gives him *zero* encouragement whatsoever. Conie tells me she's starting to feel hounded and harangued.

I don't know what her perfect man might look like, but it's not Doug Robinson. Nevertheless, Miss Mittie and even Bamie *shove* her, none too subtly, into Doug's open arms.

I say little back to her, but I nod in mute commiseration, returning her desperate, clutching hugs with a pat-pat-pat of my own against her slender back.

Conie is starting to move far beyond me now, deep into the outer atmosphere of adulthood … where I've not been invited to venture just yet. I still feel like such a child—untested, untried, and unplucked—but not for lack of trying (yes, I did just write that. No, I don't care—it's true, and I'd say it again if asked).

Will anyone ever want me? Will Theo ever tire of Alice and urge me to "come home" to his arms?

I don't think I'll write again in this journal until I have something happy to write about. And that might take a mighty long time.

Friday

26 September 1879

According to this morning's edition of the *Times*, three *million* dollars' worth of property in Deadwood, Dakota Territory just went up in a roaring conflagration in the middle of the night. I can't even imagine such a number as "one million," let alone something burning that's worth that much money!

They say more than 2,000 citizens are homeless now, with 300 buildings burned. The fire alarm first sounded at 3:30 a.m. in the wee hours when a coal oil lamp—somehow—fell off a table and onto the floor at the Empire Bakery. (I'm guessing a cat nudged it accidentally. Lamps don't fall off tables and onto the floor by themselves.)

Theo will be doubly upset at this news—not only feeling sorrow for the residents of Deadwood but because he's always feared that "something will happen to the Wild West" before he can get out there in person and see it for himself!

I wouldn't mind exploring the beauties of the west myself … with or without Theo. (But it would be vastly more fun with him than without him.)

Thursday

16 October 1879

Conie tells me that Theo (and I quote her) "stands nineteenth in his class, which began with 230 fellows." He still spends loads of time with "the fellows," driving around in a four-in-hand with his gang up to Frank Goodman's farm, where they spend the day target-shooting at glass balls.

I guess this counts as "something happy to write about."

Sort of.

No, actually, it doesn't.

Perhaps I Will

WEDNESDAY

22 OCTOBER 1879

In this morning's *New York World* newspaper—we generally subscribe to the daily *Times* and the *World,* both—I see that our own local genius, Thomas Alva Edison, finally got a filament of carbonized thread to burn … *without stopping!* … for thirteen and a half *hours* before it finally fizzled out. Oh, he's getting close now—it's only a matter of time! Why, I could read, and read, and read—all *night long* if I wanted to—with such a useful, miraculous light as that!

It was only last year that Edison formed the Edison Electric Light Company, right here in New York City, with additional investments by several bigwigs, including J. P. Morgan, Spencer Trask, and the Vanderbilt family. Remember, just because their company name includes the words "electric light" doesn't necessarily mean they *have* one that works … not just yet—but they will, you'll see! I keep following him in the papers. It's bound to happen. After all, he has that fancy scientific laboratory now in Menlo Park, New

Jersey … the one built using money from the sale of Edison's own "multiplex telegraphic system," which means he can send two messages at the same time. This local inventor/businessman has only just begun to actualize his genius in many dazzling ways.

TUESDAY

28 OCTOBER 1879

Something seems amiss with Theo—and that could be *very* good news for me.

Here it is. It's the day after Theo's twenty-first birthday, and he's *not* at Chestnut Hill for a change. Alice was not by his side on his special day either, but thank goodness his adoring family was. They were all together again in Cambridge, and today, Bamie admits to me that, "Theo seemed very happy about that, all things considered." (And by "things considered," I knew she meant on-again, off-again Alice.)

Conie also adds to me with a shrug, "He never fails to mention that, *thank heaven*, his 'actions to date' have not dishonored dear Father. I'm not sure which action he's talking about exactly, but it *must* be some sort of … of … well, irresistible blandishment, too strong for him *not* to succumb to it eventually, whatever it may be. But at least he says he's still 'pure'—can you just imagine?"

The sisters have a good laugh over that, while I merely smile like the Mona Lisa.

Dear Journal, as you will no doubt surmise on your own, Theo did *not* ask me to join the family for his twenty-first birthday celebration. I wasn't expecting an invitation, and none was forthcoming.

However, I *did* send him a small present the day before—a pair of elegant pens with gold-plated nibs. I signed the card: "To TR, from his sincere friend Edith Kermit Carow."

After all, two can play that game.

Thursday
31 October 1879

The Roosevelt sisters tell me that their brother hasn't "mentioned Alice at *all* lately, except once in a list of his guests for an opera party on 16 October."

Bamie admits that, yes, Theo still goes over to Chestnut Hill to "see friends," but these are *other* friends and ostensibly *not* Alice ... who remains yet cool, aloof, and mysterious.

I wonder...

Friday
31 October 1879

At least I still have *some* things of my own ... some *life* of my own, friends of my own, and plans of my own. So, tonight, I host my annual Halloween "girls party," just like I've done for the past ten years or more. It helps lift me out of my blue misery and does me no end of *good*.

Most of the "regulars" from years past are still around to show up, thank goodness. Yes, there are several engagements amongst the girls, but no weddings have torn us asunder just yet.

At the party tonight, Bamie tells me that Alice is deep into planning her coming-out party—already scheduled for early November. Then she'll be fair game for all the eligible men of Boston.

Bamie adds, "Dear Teedie is busy arranging family gatherings for us all to meet Alice, and he must be desperate, poor fellow! He's already arranged four such meetings over the next twenty days!"

Desperate indeed, he's not one to go down without a fight.

I'm *glad* I'm continuing my old tradition of a Girls' Halloween Party because it makes me feel like a carefree young *girl* again, for a change. I laugh more frequently, harder, and longer than I have in *ever* so many months! Even Conie laughs and "gushes" over everything, just like the olden days with her effusive old non-nervous self.

Em's exuberance with "apple-bobbing" leads to soaking the front of her dress, from neck to hem . This only made us all laugh harder, even Em.

Laughter! I didn't know I need that so desperately.

Many old friends are getting engaged these days, pairing off, moving away, and even planning their weddings. I'm all too aware that nearly all of these girls' families have far more money than mine. Although the dowry system is dying out—it's decidedly passé—it is still the expected thing for a young woman to bring a substantive financial gift to her new husband—and/or his family—when she marries.

Em seems to enjoy herself at the party—and I'm *glad*. She's just as out of sorts as I am these days—just in a different way. Just before bedtime, she even comes into my bedroom and lolls about on the foot of my bed as we giggle over the party events. There's so little these days that makes her happy—it worries me...

Sunday Night

2 November 1879

I've been distressingly ill all day long—all right, I'll say it more plainly. I've been vomiting: first my breakfast and then, later, my lunch as well. I can't keep anything down.

The reason? It's not the flu. It's because the lady in question, who I privately call Miss "Sunshine" Lee, is actually coming—*here*, in person, to Manhattan, *today*, along with one of her sisters and both parents—to stay at the Roosevelt house. Overnight.

And for a few days thereafter.

I *know* I'll be meeting her in the flesh. Despite all gossip, things do *not* sound like Theo and Alice are putting their relationship "asunder."

It sounds like the ploy of a desperate man or a calculated risk he's willing to take. It's one that probably will pay off for him in the end.

Wednesday
5 November 1879

I hear that Miss Mittie absolutely "adores" Alice and that everyone had a *grand* time together.

I do not comment about this to the Roosevelt girls or to Miss Mittie.

It is no longer my business. I keep my mouth shut and paste on that cheerful smile back on my face, at least as cheerful as I can manage.

Friday
14 November 1879

Wonderful news! (At least, wonderful for me…)

Conie says that, "Alice is colder than ever, and poor Teedie is so frustrated! Do you know how he puts it? He keeps muttering about 'the changeableness of the female mind!'"

I suspect Theo is going nearly crazy at the thought of losing Alice to another man—forever. The perfidy of Alice is driving him mad—I just know it.

But he continues to study harder than ever and never lets "the fellows" know that his heart is full of pain.

Oh, if she would *only* tell him no and be *done* with it! Why does she drag matters on and on? Is he only to be a conquest?

Saturday

15 November 1879

I *could* kick myself for mooning over Theo so much these days, but I *won't*—instead, this afternoon, I ask Papa if we can check for cheap seats tonight for *Across the Atlantic*, a new, sentimental, musical extravaganza that opened mid-October at the Olympic Theater on Broadway. You never have to ask Papa twice about going to the theater!

I *love* going to the theater with Papa, especially to the Olympic—it's actually the fourth theater building to occupy that spot. They keep building fancier edifices, tearing down the old ones for something new and shiny! This latest version of the Olympic is about ten years old; it's handsome and sumptuous. Built for (and by) the Tammany Society—the powerful Democratic political "machine" that rules most of New York City—the building has an auditorium big enough to hold public meetings (for politics) and a smaller auditorium that holds the actual theatre. These days, Tammany Hall smoothly blends (crooked) politics and entertainment together in its impressive new headquarters. There's only one small room for the Tammany Society itself. The rest of the above-ground rooms are rented out to entertainers: Don Bryant's Minstrels, a German theater company, classical concerts, and opera. The basement offers up a French restaurant called Café Ausant where Papa and I can watch *tableaux vivant* ("living pictures"), gymnastic exhibitions, pantomimes, and "Punch and Judy" shows, or all of them at once. There's also a gentlemen's bar, a bazaar for families, a Ladies' Café, and what they call an oyster saloon. Accessibility to all of this—with the exception of Bryant's—is open from seven until midnight for a combination price of just fifty cents. *Fifty cents!* You can be sure that Papa and I spend even more time down here than we did for the entire performance of *Across the Atlantic*!

Papa tells me he's heard businessmen talk about how the notorious vaudeville entertainer Tony Pastor is trying to take over the lease on the Olympic so he can make it New York's most popular new vaudeville house. We shall see…

Monday

17 November 1879

Theo hangs onto his position as vice president of the Natural History Society, no matter how Alice detests mice, spiders, and bugs. From what the girls tell me these days, T is still terribly, *terribly* afraid Alice is going to tell him *no* … while *I* pray hourly for her to do that very thing.

SUNDAY MORNING

16 NOVEMBER 1879

H*eaven.*

I'm in absolute, glorious *heaven* just now because Theo will soon be "calling" on me. I guess that's going to mean he'll be "speaking properly" to me again.

Yes, you heard correctly. He'll be "calling" as a proper gentleman should.

Via written note, he invited me to stroll with him today through our very favorite park, Riverside, and then to dine with him afterward at Delmonico's, the exquisite, urbane restaurant everyone is mad about these days.

So there's hope for me—for *us*—yet.

More details to come later. All I can say now is … thank you, thank you, and yet again *thank you*. I'm thanking God, destiny, and divine providence. All of these, working together, will finally make our story come right.

Hope … it's a wonderful thing.

Sunday night

16 November 1879

My hope now lies bleeding, slain not by Teedie's words but by his deeds.

Early on, everything today was heavenly. It was *perfect.*

Too perfect, I'm thinking now—it's never perfect, I guess, when the smile on one's face is of the tremulous sort. My face was no doubt glowing with foolish love of him.

We strolled … we talked … we dined … and we *laughed*. Oh yes, like ninnies! We shared big horse laughs that came from the bottoms of our bellies. I mentioned how November in Manhattan has always been the happiest of months for me … the happiest of times and places … and he didn't disagree. After a lovely Delmonico's early dinner, he walks me home. Although we don't hold hands, we still smile at one another as we walk. We smile a lot, meaningfully. (At least, my smile is meaningful toward *him*.)

As we stand together—on the top step of the stoop before my front door—he commences talking but in halting tones: "Edith,"—Not Edie, just Edith—"Edith, you are *still* the most cultivated and best-read girl I've ever known."

Then, I take a breath and say something I shouldn't.

"Oh, assuredly Alice must be very well-read, too. You know you only go for girls who like books!" I laugh—only it sounds more like the bleating of a little lost lamb.

"Truth be told, Alice goes in more for tennis than for books," Theo admits with his handsome, toothsome grin.

Then he continues, and the blow falls. My hope dies with it.

"Speaking of Alice, I'd better get along home now. Motherling, Nell, the girls, and I are all taking the evening train to Cambridge—tonight, as it happens!—to spend a couple of days at Chestnut Hill. So I'd best say thank you for your company—and … goodbye for now, Edith."

And—smiling an enigmatic, lopsided smile—he extends his hand to me.

He wants me to shake his hand.

So I do.

Then I enter my house … make a flimsy excuse to Mamma, Papa, and Em … trudge up to my room …

… and proceed to cry, and cry, and cry.

Nothing has changed in Theo's attitude toward me, except more kindness and civility.

Nothing else will ever change.

His no is respectful, but it's a *real* no—I know that now.

I must make my way into the wilderness of my future alone.

Saturday

22 November 1879

Finally! The staff at Newsboys' Lodging House has at last given me official permission to occasionally "help serve" the half-grown "boy-businessmen" at their rollicking suppers. Along with two other society women (much older than I, ladies I'd never met before), we're there tonight on our culinary maiden voyage. Our evening consists of "prep and cooking" (making boiled cabbage with salt pork under the sharp eye of Mrs. O'Flaherty, an old Irish woman and longtime cook), "serving" (dishing-out food as each newsboy comes down the line, thrusting their plates toward us with both hands, ear-to-ear grins on each face), and then us society belles "washing up."

These days, male Irish lads who become newsboys have a slight, new swagger (not too much, just enough) and *plenty* of confidence (almost, but not quite cheeky), all because of the ragingly popular *Ragged Dick* book series.

The first time I volunteered for the newsboys—that time when I was told to "stay in the kitchen" until such time as I became "authorized to work and serve"—I was so surprised to glimpse the so-called "ragged boys" as they milled about by the open kitchen door.

Perhaps I Will

They all laughed and joked with one another, so free-and-easy, light, and cheerful.

Until I saw them up close, I thought they'd be sad, grimy little things, downtrodden and miserable. And probably they *were* ... back in the day ... back before *Ragged Dick* and the construction of the Newsboys' Lodging House, this place of their salvation.

These days, newsboys act as if they're members of a special club that supports and nurtures them in their aspirations to become successful, influential businessmen and universally admired as noble.

People say the *Ragged Dick* books are even *more* popular than the Dickens novels of twenty years back and that the new book series has drawn abreast of, or even surpassed, Dickens for worldwide popularity. (At Miss Comstock's, I recall how we learned that people would actually go down to meet ships coming in from England just to buy the latest installment of *The Old Curiosity Shop* to see if Little Nell had died or survived. Hint: Alas, her "arduous journey" did her in.)

But now it's Horatio Alger Jr. and "his newsboys" who are all the rage. All of the English-speaking world—and I'm not exaggerating, *truly* I'm not—knows of the phenomenally best-selling *Ragged Dick* books. Alger continues to crank them out as fast as he can before his readers grow weary of him (as they inevitably will). I think he's up to nine books so far in this particular series.

Since I was coming back to serve frequently at the Newsboys' Lodging House, I figured I'd better discover what all the hoopla was about the *Ragged Dick* books. I did a very daring thing for a young lady of good breeding and proper family, and I (surreptitiously!) bought two used copies of Alger's books from a second-hand book dealer. I decided to choose book four (the best-selling *Ragged Dick*), along with the latest installment, book ten, the smartly selling *Rough and Ready.*

I did *not* show the Alger books to *anyone* at home, of course. Grandfather Tyler would break out into apoplexy if he heard I was reading "popular trash." I keep the books hidden under my mattress atop the tightly strung ropes. Even though Alger's books are earnest, clean, and upright—nothing at all to be ashamed of—they are the furthest thing from "fine literature." (Maybe that's why they're so popular.)

Ragged Dick, the story of a poor boy's rise to middle-class respectability, was, and still is, a roaring success—I think everyone in America owns at least one copy and keeps adding new books in the series to their collections.

Tonight (before writing in this journal), I read an hour out of *Rough and Ready,* which tells the story of a poor New York newsboy (what else?) called by the nickname "Rough and Ready" who struggles to support his little sister while protecting her from their abusive stepfather. So far, the story is a regular "rouser." Even Alger's titles are enough to chirk up one's courage and keep going in the face of adversity: *Adrift in New York ... Do and Dare or a Brave Boy's Fight for Fortune ... Struggling Upward ... Risen from the Ranks ... Hector's Inheritance ...*

and so many more. They all run together after a while...

The Horatio Alger myth that most people accept as gospel is that stalwart newsboys *can* (and do) become wealthy simply through noble hard work and putting one's nose to the grindstone.

But I don't believe it for one *minute*.

Even just by reading two Alger books so far, I see a flaw in that premise—bewitching and irresistible as it may yet be. The poor but noble newsboys do *not* find success by simply working hard. In the Alger books, the cause of the boy's ultimate success is *actually* "a lucky break" that works to the boy's advantage. For instance, it could be rescuing a rich person from an overturned carriage who then gives him a handsome reward ... or the newsboy might return a large sum of "lost money" to the rightful owner ... something (improbable) along those lines. After the critical "lucky break," the ragged but noble newsboy conducts himself admirably with honesty, industriousness, and altruism. This inevitably brings the newsboy—and his plight—to the attention of another wealthy individual who either adopts him or sets him up in business with a vision of a glorious, well-earned future.

But what about the newsboys—or indeed any of the regular people who daily toil—who do *not* experience a "lucky break?" What then?

What indeed?

Well, despite the "holes in their plots," the *Ragged Dick* books are great fun to read. Plus, they serve a great purpose of encouraging countless poor newsboys to "soldier on into the fray." They may yet find their dreams fulfilled. After all, anything can happen in America, and it *sometimes* does in the most astonishing of ways.

Sunday

23 November 1879

Apparently, the Roosevelt family's recent visit to Chestnut Hill was *such* a resounding success that Theo arranged for what is properly termed a "four-plate luncheon" for thirty at the Porcellian Club at Harvard—a shocking expense that even Theo can ill afford!—to which the "family elders" of the Roosevelt, Lee, and Saltonstall clans were individually invited.

Additional gossip I have straight from Conie's latest letter: "Teedie also invited the most alluring of his Boston girlfriends and the most fashionable of 'the fellows' to eke out the remaining places around the huge table, and, well, all three families are just thick as thieves, now! It's as if we've all known and loved one another *forever*—isn't that grand?"

Her words speak for themselves, and I've neither the will nor energy for comment.

Thursday — Thanksgiving Day
27 November 1879

What of us Carows on this Thanksgiving Day, 1879? For the past few days, Mamma and Papa have taken to their respective beds: Mamma because she fears she's coming down with symptoms of the membranous croup and Papa because work opportunities—even at the family shipping business—are even skimpier and more discouraging of late. He's been "sweetening" his bourbon with laudanum.

And me?

I've covered my ongoing artwork with old sheets for a while … put aside my poetry and essays (it gives me a headache just to think of it) … and, oddly enough, I've been spending much time lately with Emily and her lessons.

Usually, Em and Mamma spend a couple of hours each day droning over English grammar, the English poets, and French recitations (using old, battered textbooks that I was able to surreptitiously buy from Miss Comstock's School at the end of the term), but now, neither of our parents feels up to the task of teaching Em.

I've always felt silently guilty over the fact of my successful graduation from (and prepaid tuition for) Miss Comstock's School, while poor, whining, giggling, and aggravating Em had to learn lessons on her own at home, with only Mamma to help her.

Earlier on, when Em and I tried studying together, we ended up arguing over stupid things and retreating to our own rooms.

I know that Em attempted the entrance exams for Miss Comstock's a couple of times, but each time, she failed miserably. Even Grandfather Tyler's influence couldn't sneak her in.

Anyway, with Mamma feeling sick and with Papa feeling ... indisposed ... I left Mame to gently care for my parents—as only dear, loyal Mame knows how best to do—and I drag Emily with me to assist the other volunteers with turkey dinner and festivities at No. 9 Duane Street, the Newsboys' Lodging House.

Dinner is slated for late afternoon there, and what a jolly affair it is, filled with much thankful chewing, slurping, and hilarious anecdotes. Because Em and I are both females, of course we aren't allowed—for propriety's sake—to "sit amongst the boys," even though most are much younger than us. But we can and do "cook and serve" them, making light conversations with them in the course of our duties.

The cooks kindly make up heaping plates for Em, myself, and other society women helpers in the kitchen afterward. Along with the other volunteering ladies, Em and I pull up stools along the kitchen drainboard and gratefully devour the good food on our plates.

For a little while at least, *we*—I think I can speak for us both, Em and I—*we feel* happily *alive* again. It takes so little, really, to bring a smile to our faces: a grinning, grateful newsboy (I want to hug them all!) or overtures of kindness from a society lady standing next to me grating carrots. Happiness can come from the most surprising of places, for which I am deeply grateful.

On the "Theo front," he is still slouching about at Chestnut Hill, no doubt fawning over Alice (as much as she will allow him) during this family holiday together. No doubt, Alice is also driving Theo over the edge of sanity with her dithering indecision.

Did I also mention that Theo started to write a book? Its provisional title is *The Naval War of 1812*. It's a weighty subject for a callow College Fellow, but, after all, no subject is too daunting or off-limits for Theo. Despite his worries about losing Alice and the endless "pegging away" at his studies, Theo always manages to find something of value to do, study, create … and become.

Wednesday night

3 December 1879

I have it on the highest authority (from Conie) that, just four days after Thanksgiving, Alice Hathaway Lee, known far and wide as Sunshine, finally celebrated her "coming out" into society with a *lavish* party in Cambridge. Yes, the traditional "shower of rosebuds" was everywhere evident.

Or so I was told—I wasn't there, of course.

Eligible men now swarm around Alice like wasps to a honey-pot. Poor Theo … I can almost empathize with his dilemma—almost, but not quite.

A friend of the Roosevelt family sent a letter to Miss Mittie today that speaks to Theo's innate determination and resolve.

Apparently, Theo continues to run doggedly with the pack of eligible men who currently encircle Alice. He can scarcely conceal his frustration. "See that girl?" he exclaimed to an acquaintance recently at a Hasty Pudding function, pointing across the room toward Alice. "I am going to marry her. She won't have me, but I am going to have *her!*"

My heart demurs: *surely* that cannot happen. Things could not get *that* far. It's outside of the realm of possibility.

I refuse to consider otherwise because down that path lies—for me—only despair.

Saturday

20 December 1879

Here I am at the Roosevelt home today to ostensibly deliver a couple of modest Christmas presents to the girls. Neither Bamie nor Conie happen to be home today—although Elliott is, and he greets me warmly at the door and remains, chatting companionably for a while.

Then, he looks sheepish (and a bit embarrassed) while he says, "Excuse me just a moment, will you? I'll be right back." I see him heading toward the "necessary," and while he is "unavoidably detained," I step as close as I dare to the open parlor door to hear what Uncle James West Roosevelt might be divulging to his sister-in-law, Miss Mittie.

Their faces look *so* serious and fraught … I just *know* there has to be something bad happening with Theo.

Here is what I glean from my shocking, subversive behavior.

Apparently, Theo's chronic insomnia has recently worsened, so dangerously that he's stopped sleeping altogether. He's even stopped "trying to pretend" and refuses to even go to bed at *all*.

Instead, he's taken to wandering … endlessly, aimlessly, all through the night … through the frozen woods around Cambridge. Perhaps he dozes a bit during the day—Uncle James doesn't say. But I *do* know Theo cannot keep this up—this ceaseless, sleepless wandering—and remain healthy.

Two nights ago, on his way to his nightly peregrinations into the forest, Theo happens to run into a friend of his, the college-age son of one of the directors of the Bank of Massachusetts. (I forget the name Uncle James mentions, and it doesn't matter anyway.)

The young fellow is shocked at Theo's gaunt pallor, red-rimmed eyes, and near incoherence. The friend *begs* Theo to allow him to "return him to his flat and to … please, *please!* … just get into bed for a little while."

Theo refuses.

So the classmate sends a telegram to Theo's family that very night—he is afraid Theo is losing his mind and endangering his life.

Fortunately, Uncle James happens to be in Cambridge on business, and after more family telegrams pass back and forth, James rushes to the aid of his stricken nephew.

Somehow, in the midst of all this, the distraught, young, love-sick Theo is treated by a sensible doctor and given calming medication and some soothing, friendly advice from Uncle James. Theo finally returns to his bed and something approaching a normal sleep schedule.

For the time being, Theo has been urged to *not* see Alice *at all* during the two weeks before Christmas vacation. Instead, he's to let his nerves subside, soothe, rest, and rejuvenate.

I am shaken to the core to hear such news. I knew things were serious about Theo's state of mind, but not *this* serious—nothing that would endanger his *life*, for heaven's sake.

Perhaps I Will

When Elliott returns from the "necessary," I make my excuses to him and plead that "I must run, Mamma is waiting for me"… leaving Miss Mittie and Uncle James still talking *sotto voce* to one another in the parlor.

I stalk home, slowly but deliberately, like an automaton whose eyes see only inwardly.

Monday

22 December 1879

Conie comes by my house to reciprocate with gifts of her own for me—and something for Em as well so she won't feel left out. Then Conie blurts happily, "Theo came home this noon for Christmas vacation—none the worse for wear, thank *God!*"

I exhale then, weak with relief and joy.

I know Conie means every fervent word she says about Theo.

She loves her brother dearly. Jealously.

Both Roosevelt sisters, Mother Mittie, and Elliott were literally worried *sick* by Theo's nervous state of mind.

But now their older brother is back, seemingly back to his old self again. All is right with the world again—almost.

Midnight on Christmas Eve

24 December 1879

What a magical night! It's silent, sacred. Flakes fall slowly, as big and lacy as hand-crocheted doilies.

As is Theo's Christmas Eve custom (ever since he was old enough to simultaneously walk and talk), he spends all afternoon and evening "paying Christmas Eve calls on ten different friends"—most of whom *also* happen to be "girls" … friend girls … girlfriends … and pretty, too.

These calls are very brief—fifteen minutes at most—but are hugely enjoyed by both the caller and each recipient, only too thrilled to receive some of the caller's voluble Christmas cheer.

But Theo's last "call" of the night on Christmas Eve … was with *me*.

I could hardly believe it. I trembled with joy and couldn't stop smiling. Maybe this *means* something … maybe Alice is ancient history now … maybe?…

For more than an hour, we walk and talk together—smiling, always smiling—through the cold darkness. Up and down the silent, snowy streets of Manhattan, we walk. In the distance, bells tolls for the 10 p.m. service at the Fifth Avenue Presbyterian Church.

As our Christmas Eve walk concludes and we approach my front door, I think for a moment … for one brief second … that he might actually kiss me.

But he doesn't.

However, he squeezes my hands in both of his. "Merry Christmas, Edith," he says.

And I reply, "Merry Christmas, Theodore."

Then he flashes me a private, dazzling smile as I reluctantly close the door between us.

CHRISTMAS DAY MORNING
25 DECEMBER 1879

This is a day for church and family. I know I shan't see Theo today, but that's all right.

Because he's invited me to have lunch at the elegant Delmonico's Restaurant—yet again!—on Boxing Day tomorrow.

He ... doesn't seem *quite* back to his old loving self just yet ... but I hope, and I *trust*, that he's making his own, deliberate way back to normal life between us—and to love.

FRIDAY
26 DECEMBER 1879

Lunch at elegant Delmonico's is everything dreamy as it should be...

Perhaps I Will

…until Theo blurts out, "Uh, by the way, just so you'll know, we're greeting some house guests tonight, and they'll be staying here a full week! It's Alice Lee, her younger sister Rosy, and her cousins Dick and Rose Saltonstall … all coming to stay here in town. The girls and dear Motherling are beside themselves with joy! You'll get to meet her too, of course. We're planning a brunch so she can meet everyone while she's here."

I just blink at him for the longest time. I can scarcely make my lips form words. "Well! A … house party. What fun for you. And for Alice, too, of course."

I smile, but the smile does not reach my eyes.

SATURDAY

27 DECEMBER 1879

I can't *bear* to meet her in person: Alice. I just can't.
But I *must*.

Momentum shoots me along in its millrace, and I see that I'm soon *going* to meet Alice—whether I want to or not.

Over the last couple of days, Conie and Bamie have regaled me with news of Theo and Alice "sleighing through Central Park, isn't that romantic?" and evenings of formal dinners and dance parties as Theo squires Alice all around Manhattan. His delight in doing so seems boundless.

He keeps marveling to his sisters, "Alice's presence here at West 57th seems so ... so natural! Don't you feel it, too?" What does that make *me?* Unnatural? Or someone so beyond "natural" as to be boring and commonplace—unworthy of any significance? It doesn't bear thinking about.

Perhaps I Will

Sunday

28 December 1879

Today, I'll be setting eyes on Alice Lee officially for the very first time. (My boxing match viewing of her seems like a fever dream now—and what if it wasn't Alice after all?)

We're to meet at a twenty-person brunch/reception at the Roosevelt's at eleven this morning. I'll find out then if she's one and the same.

Oh, I'm going to be *sick*—

Or will I feel like slapping her, instead? Will I fall down in a faint? Cry or recoil from her?

More on this later—all details will become evident, once it all starts happening.

LATER today:

I don't vomit, faint, recoil, or weep.

Instead, an odd, brittle "presence of mind" settles over me—like floating bits of hoarfrost that burn and freeze me simultaneously—just before Alice and Theo appear before me as a smiling couple, ready for me to introduce myself.

Yes, Alice is one and the same: the same gorgeous girl I observed at Theo's boxing match.

At first glance, my eyes are drawn to her elaborately "marcelled" blonde hair—the height of fashion, of course, created by the skill of a lady's maid via special curling tongs invented by Monsieur Marcel himself, the famous French hairdresser.

I then take in her other attributes: her slender figure, tall yet undeniably athletic; her innocent smile—assuming friendship and acceptance wherever she may be; and her crystal blue eyes—obviously curious about me, yet always confident and happy with herself and her world.

Alice possesses all the attractiveness of the girl I remembered at the boxing match—only now, up close, her beauties are amplified tenfold.

No wonder Theo is bewitched.

The only thing I don't admire about her is her eyes. They look like ghost eyes to me, pale gray-blue crystals that look back at me from another world.

Somehow, I make it through the brunch, smiling and chatting—and hiding my trembling hands under the table when not using them to daintily make use of my fork, spoon, or knife.

I observe Alice for—how shall I say this? Signs of coarseness? A bad temperament (or bad breath)? A shallow mind or mean spirit?

I must honestly report that Alice evinces *none* of these behaviors. Instead, she radiates sunshine back upon us all, enlivened by ripples of ready, gay laughter.

Truly, she lives up to her nickname—Sunshine. With unabashed, toothsome adoration, Theo can't take his eyes off her.

A dispassionate-but-still-curious part of my brain wonders whether Sunshine will hold up during the rest of her visit. Will she be just as irresistible to the group at the end of the week … as she is today?

Wednesday
31 December 1879

Edison's "miracle lights" are for real now—what a wonder! Today was the very first day the American public was actually invited to *see* the wonder, glory, and practical applications of incandescent lighting, *and*—thanks to Christmas gift train tickets from Grandfather Tyler on the Pennsylvania Railroad from NYC to Menlo Park, New Jersey, we Carows set out on a marvelous "field trip" (so to speak) to see this wonderful sight for ourselves. In Menlo Park, an entire street—up and down several blocks—is now fitted with incandescent lighting. The electric lamps will be lit at 4 p.m. and remain lit, all night long, until 7 a.m. the following New Year's Day.

In response to great public enthusiasm before the event, the Pennsylvania Railroad Company are running special "Edison's Light" trains to Menlo Park all afternoon and evening on the day of the demonstration.

Perhaps I Will

After the thirty-three-mile train ride from Grand Central Terminal (actually, I think they're calling it Grand Central Station these days), Papa, Mamma, Mame, Em, and I all held hands and were careful to *not* get separated. Yes, the mobs of excited people were *that large* and enthusiastic. Walking over from the train station (with many hundreds of people ahead of us, many hundreds behind, and more coming every minute), before we even get to the lit-up street, I can hear high-pitched oooohs and ahhhhs from the crowds, as if watching a fireworks display. And then we're finally there!

We see a whole row of handsome, Italianate lamps, affixed to poles at intervals, all up and down the streets, for many blocks into the distance. It was such a steady, golden light—so beautiful, constant, efficient, scientific, and wonderful. Their light seems to brighten and grow the darker it becomes.

Truly … *truly,* this new decade of the '80s … 1880 and beyond … can only bring good things to us all. (That is my fervent prayer, anyway.)

Papa has to finally pull me away from the enchanting spectacle. He reminds me that Mamma's back hurts, Mame looks totally exhausted, and Em makes fretful noises about finding dinner somewhere, so we make our way back to the Menlo Park station and board the next train. The clickety-clack of the train wheels soon make us all drowsy but not too sleepy so we didn't know enough to get out at Grand Central Station. We're still awake enough to hire a "growler" cab, instead of a two-seated hansom to squeeze in five people, which takes us home to our slightly dodgy neighborhood.

It's the best New Year's Eve I can ever remember! Thank you, Grandfather Tyler, and bless your heart!

Friday

2 January 1880

New Year's Day, 1880, dawned calm and sunny. All day long, I kept waiting—

and hoping—for an invitation from Theo ... a handwritten note delivered by one of his servants, maybe ... asking me to join his house party for New Year's Day festivities.

But ... no.

I receive nothing. Hear nothing.

Now, on the following day, I *do* receive a hand-delivered note. I hold my breath in anticipation—but it's just a note from Conie, full of chat and romantic gossip. (Conie writes that I'd "probably be interested." Um, yes, quite probably...)

Conie reports that, on New Year's Day, her family takes out two closed carriages for a drive, all the way to the racetrack at Jerome Park for lunch. Then, they spend the afternoon dancing at the truly magnificent ballroom in the racetrack's clubhouse. Conie comes right out and says it: Alice looks *truly* enchanting in his arms! But the Boston Bunch—which now includes Theo—will be on the train early tomorrow morning, back to college and/or their usual pursuits. Even Elliott heads back to his military institute tomorrow.

And *so*.

Just like that, they are off and gone.

Life seems frighteningly quiet without their happy bustle and din.

I still feel the brittle, fragile hoarfrost crystals drift down upon my body ... more and more of them all the time ... burning.

With nothing to be done about assuaging the pain.

What *can* I do but endure it and keep on keeping on. Besides, the golden glow of spending New Year's Eve in Menlo Park with the incandescent lights still warms my heart and "chirks" me up. I aim to keep on as I always do—managing our household bills; reassuring Mamma that she doesn't have a new, loathsome disease; comforting Papa with daughterly attention and company at the theater where even the "cheap seats" bring us both great enjoyment; being decent and sisterly to Em (even when she's infuriating and pitiful); and continuing to perform good deeds at the same charities where Greatheart used to spread his most welcomed benevolence.

Perhaps I Will

Sunday

1 February 1880

It's the bad old month of February again—the month when dear Greatheart died after so much suffering. Nothing good *ever* happens for Roosevelts—or to *me* either, an honorary Roosevelt to my way of thinking—during the ominous, gloomy month of February.

But Theo is home again this weekend—a total surprise to everyone—and, as Bamie divulged to me Friday, "He's home for just the day to go shopping!"

Shopping!? What new madness can *this* be?

I'm well aware Theo has a weakness for fashionable attire. Is he trying to allure Alice with the brilliance and cut of a new waistcoat?

I'm off now to join Aunt Annie Gracie, Conie, Bamie, and Miss Mittie for Sunday afternoon tea and cakes at their house. Will write more about that later…

I do have a present for Theo, though … it's the first issue *ever* of the new journal *Science*,

February 1880, with financial backing from Thomas Edison. I will mail it to his Harvard address. Surely he will enjoy and treasure this. Surely he will think of me when he reads it. *Surely...*

LATER tonight:

It's official: Theo and Alice are getting *married*.

It all started with the letter Bamie handed me at the ladies' tea today. When I arrived, I found that Miss Mittie and Conie had already sent their regrets—due to sudden, roiling stomachs, probably "la grippe"—and gone off to their beds (while taking turns occupying "the necessary" down the hall).

Miss Mittie previously ordered mountains of little cakes, tarts, and other dainty fare, so she told Bamie to tell us all to "Go ahead and proceed without us—and please do eat hearty!"

And so, Bamie, Aunt Annie, and I dine in solitary splendor from glass tea trays. But it's far too quiet without Miss Mittie's sweet, Southern drawl and the cheerful prattling of Conie.

Perhaps I Will

Usually, Bamie holds everyone spellbound with her mesmerizing stories, wry jokes, and natural magnetism. But today she seems distracted, as if in a hurry for all of us to eat and be done with it. We take her hint and comply as fast as we can.

Once servants remove our lap trays and the crumb-filled plates, Bamie claps her hands. "Now then! Our darling Teedie has an announcement to make. And since he's not here to make it in person, he has left letters for the two of you that explain it all. You'll probably get the idea when I tell you *why* he came home this weekend to 'go shopping:' he was shopping for an engagement ring for Alice! I *have* to be the first to tell you—she's accepted him! And Theo's over the moon with joy!"

Aunt Annie emits a sudden shriek—a mixture of shock, laughter, joy, and surprise. And I feel my blood turn to ice as the bottom drops out of my stomach.

Bamie hands both of us sealed letters. Aunt Annie rips hers hurriedly and read Theo's unmistakable handwriting. "Oh my *goodness*, dear *heaven* … The boy has gone and *done* it!"

Annie and Bamie clutch one another's hands, laughing, crying, and shrieking in very unladylike ways. Bamie adds more of her own editorial comments: "Yes, it feels rather sudden, but Brother is *so* smitten—and we've all come to love Alice dearly. She gave Mother the most *touching* letter, I just can't tell you how lovely it was…"

Hoarfrost shimmers over me, again and again. It burns like fire and keeps on burning. How shall I ever stand it, how—

"Read your letter, Edie! See what he says." Aunt Annie and Bamie clamor at me to open the envelope that rests in my sweaty, quivering hand.

With trembling fingers, I manage to open the letter and unfold the single sheet of paper within.

I read the letter silently. I try to keep my face from looking like the open book that it is.

(Yes, of *course*, I keep the letter. I fold it carefully and put it into the pocket of my skirt.

But I cannot look at it again. For as long as I *live*, I'll never look at it again.)

It's a short letter. Even though I'll never read it again, I'll never forget it either:

1 February 1880
Dearest Edith,
I wanted to tell you … first (this word is underlined) before anyone else I know—except, of course, our immediate Roosevelt family—about our joyful news. Miss Alice Hathaway Lee accepted my proposal of marriage, and we shall wed in Brookline, Massachusetts, on my twenty-second birthday, October 27, 1880. We hope you will join us at our wedding celebration at the First Unitarian Church in Brookline on that date. With great joy and inestimable respect for our long and special relationship, I shall remain your friend always,

Theodore Roosevelt II

Seconds are passing … then minutes, but I am still frozen. I can scarcely breathe. I *know* my face is an open book for all. But I *can't* let them know how much I'm aching inside. They mustn't *ever* know. Else how could I live with myself?

For sixteen years, I've shared Theo's life (oh God, oh *Teedie*) … in our little home-school together on the second floor of Teedie's house … shared his home life, many of his vacations, ditto his dreams and desires.

I *know* shock and pain is written all over my face, but I can't help it.

From very far away, I hear Aunt Annie's soft voice close to my ear. "Are you all right, dear heart? You look about to faint."

I see Bamie looking at me in surprise and consternation. Aunt Annie's face is sweetly soft and worried as she looks at me.

Nobody knows what to do.

Certainly not I.

But then I hear someone speaking in a high, thin, reedy voice. "Yes, I'm all right…" (I'm surprised that it's me. I feel like a spirit is speaking through me, using my mouth, like at a seance.) "That is, I *will* be all right shortly … but, actually, I think I'd best go home now. Mamma will be wondering what's keeping me."

(Such a silly excuse, but no one calls me on it. Surely they know that I *must* go home before I collapse in front of them.)

Aunt Annie sends a boy to find me a hansom cab—yes, it's a bit risqué for a young woman to ride in one alone, but "needs must" in such an emergency—and in short order, they send me home in style.

The last memory I have of that afternoon is seeing the resigned, pitying look on their faces.

I can't write any more about this. Not tonight.

Not ever.

Tuesday

3 February 1880

Today I'm starting to read a new novel called *Splendid Misery*.

The title speaks for itself—and for me.

Monday

16 February 1880

Theo formally announces his engagement to Alice today ... two days after Valentine's Day. (*Why* has he scheduled something so important during a month that has heretofore brought him only misery? To change the "turn of the tide," perhaps?)

The ivory-tinted card looks—and is—impressive on heavy card stock. The print is the expensive "raised" kind, not cheap letterpress.

To Theo's way of thinking, only the best is good enough for Alice.

Perhaps I Will

S ATURDAY

21 F EBRUARY 1880

Conie shares more and more of Theo's letters with me. I wish she wouldn't; they all gush so about Alice.

And what good could it *possibly* do me to have such salt sprinkled cavalierly into my wounds?

Then why does my heart climb into my throat when I see Conie take a new letter from her pocket?

Admit it, Miss Carow. You're addicted to his letters, *and* to him, even if he belongs to another.

Here are some quotes, verbatim, from recent letters from Theo to his family: "My sweet, pretty, pure queen, my laughing little love … how bewitchingly pretty she is! I cannot help petting her and caressing her all the time … she is such a perfect little Sunshine. I do not believe any man ever loved a woman more than I love her."

Oh yes … twist that knife a little more each time. Why not? The proper do-gooder

Miss Carow can obviously take it. She *has* been "taking it" for some time now without any apparent ill effects.

MONDAY

23 FEBRUARY 1880

I see it on a newsstand today while on my way to the grocer's: the *New York Daily Graphic* newspaper printed a *real picture* ... a sort of *photograph*, but not exactly ... on the front page! How they did I could hardly tell you—another miracle of science, I guess. I bought the paper for Papa—he's always interested in curiosities like this. The article about the image says it is called a "half-tone engraving." It's the first time ever in a newspaper, and there's going to be lots more in the future. Like I said, 1880 is going to be a year of surprises with something new coming down the pike every day!

Popular music is really something, too— *so* irresistible this year. We've never had so many "singable" songs all at once and everywhere. Yes, sometimes the lyrics are silly, but who can resist the likes of "Sailing, sailing, over the ocean blue!" or the dreamy waltz "Roses from the South"—and don't forget "Give me Some Time to Blow the Man Down!" (Few know what it means, but what does it matter? It's so infectious to sing!) The most irresistible of all is "Funiculi, Funicula." Nothing can match its unabashed joy as it exhorts singers to, "Listen! Listen! Music trills from afar."

How I wish I could sing these with Theo, rejoicing in his out-of-tune, enthusiastic tones as I play for us on the grand piano in his ballroom … instead of practicing these infectious songs in a solitary funk on our tinkling old upright piano in the back parlor.

I wonder if Alice can play the piano, if her voice is as sweet and clear as a nightingale's, instead of high, breathy, and squeaky like mine?

WEDNESDAY

25 FEBRUARY 1880

My sketches and paintings remain hidden under old sheets. My poems and essays lie in piles in my bottom desk drawer—unfinished, nesting material for mice perhaps.

The Lee family agreed to a wedding on Theo's birthday, October 27. I'm not surprised. I've always known that Theo can out-argue and persuade any lawyer—anytime, anywhere—and convince you that *his* decision was *your* idea all along ... leaving everyone happy (and bedazzled) in the end.

All is *not* perfect in paradise, however.

Theo seems constantly afraid that someone will "run off with dear Sunshine." His sisters tell me he's constantly "glowering darkly about fighting duels" over her. He's not speaking in jest, either. He even sent abroad for a set of French dueling pistols.

I wonder what it would feel like for two men to fight a duel over me. It's so far removed from possibility that I can't imagine any details—except as an onlooker.

Thursday

1 March 1880

Theo is finally starting to "relax."

Don't get me wrong, I'm *not* happy he's going to marry another girl.

It's just that I'm happy *he* is finally relaxed and happy ... no longer wandering sleepless all night in the woods, ordering dueling pistols, or enduring bouts of his nerve-induced illness, the cholera morebus.

Bamie reports that Alice is sweetly "behaving herself" and staying true to "dear Brother." Bamie says that Theo is resigning many of his official positions so he can spend more time with his bride-to-be.

Worst of all ... Theo quit the vice presidency of Harvard's Natural History Society. Now I *know* he's truly and deeply serious about all this.

He would *never* do this if not for the love of Alice—she who hates all bugs and snakes.

EASTER WEEKEND
28 MARCH 1880

I've just returned from a gala and private dinner in honor of Theo and Alice. Yes, they're back in Manhattan for Easter Weekend. (Evidently, I've now become part of Theo's "set" … his crowd of dinner friends—"friend enough" to stay in touch with but no longer important enough to consider for marriage.)

T wants to impress his local friends at a dinner in her honor—and impress us he does! Alice, too, is ravishing in pink and mauve silk.

At an after-dinner toast (which he conducts with lemonade—no more liquor for Theo, and I'm relieved about this for many reasons), he announces to us all: "I'm aiming to rub up your memories about the existence of a man named Theodore Roosevelt who is going to be bringing a pretty Boston wife back to New York City next winter!"

Thursday

22 April 1880

"Are you *sure* you want to keep hearing these, Edie?" Even Conie is becoming dubious of the efficacy of her continuing to "rub my nose" in the continuing adventures of Theo and Alice.

"Yes, *certain*-sure," I always tell her. "I'm *fine,* so pray do continue."

(Sometimes I even believe it myself. But when I'm being honest, I don't. I'm careful not to divulge my … how shall I call it? … my other life.)

Thus, I'm generally the first person (outside of the family) to hear highlights of Theo's latest visits to the mansion at Chestnut Hill:

Alice and Theo play tennis together—she's a crackerjack player, or so he says.

Alice embroiders while Theo reads to her from the latest books.

Alice and Theo take endless drives in his dogcart.

Evenings, they play cards together, including whist and euchre—and laugh a lot.

Before bedtime, they take an hour's walk—together, alone—in the moonlight.

Conie finishes reading Theo's latest letter with a conclusion that leaves even me speechless. "Oh, listen to this part, Edie! Get this … he writes, 'She is so far above my other girls, my pearl, my pure flower, my darling, my own best-loved little queen!'"

SO many adjectives. I'm suddenly dizzy and nauseous.

My other girls. I guess that includes me.

I can only nod in return and keep that Mona Lisa smile upon my lips.

Perhaps I Will

Thursday

13 May 1880

Edison does it again! This self-taught man is an absolute, sure-enough genius. We New Yorkers love and admire him, consider him "one of our own." Now he invented—and today conducted his first test of—an actual electric railway system. Good riddance to belching black smoke and rivers of ashes all over everybody! Just strong, clean, reliable electricity. He did the test near Menlo Park, as always, but with no public crowds watching this time. The track was about a third of a mile long, made up of lightweight rails spiked to ties which were lying right on the ground … the electric locomotive pulled three cars: a flat freight car, an open-awning car, and a boxcar called a Pullman with electromagnetic brakes. The test went smooth and perfect as can be. Now all the talk is that New York City will be having electric trains, both elevated and even subterranean, as soon as it's economically feasible. What did I tell you about the 1880s?! It's like a new renaissance of science and inventions. Nothing would surprise me now!

Tuesday
1 June 1880

Finally, a change of scene on the home front, for which I'm ready, ready, *more* than ready. We're off today to spend a month at Grandfather Tyler's summer place near the Jersey Shore. I just want to walk in the beautiful woods there and find soothing respite amid the flowering bloodroots and trilliums.

I hope it will help my malaise...

Wednesday
2 June 1880

It's helping, thank goodness.
I'm smiling again and seeing the world now as "containing more interesting possibilities" …

if not exactly actualities at present. There's hope for me yet.

Thursday
10 June 1880

Again, letters fly thick and fast between Conie and myself. She writes that Theo is signing up to study law next year as a stepping-stone into politics.

Politics! I can scarce form the word in my mind—it makes me retch to do so.

Such a dirty, nasty, sordid business ... one that killed dear Greatheart and threatens to drag Theo into the gutter, too—or worse. I can scarcely believe his choice and decision.

But Theo explains to us all, "I'm doing this to try to help the cause of better government in New York City. Of course, I don't know exactly *how* I'm going to do it just yet!"

He's already working on his senior thesis, and—wouldn't you just know—he's chosen the most controversial political subject of our day to write about: "The Practicability of Giving Men and Women Equal Rights." He has always been in favor of this throughout his entire young life, no more so than right now.

He's only just started in on this exhaustive report, but already he instructs us soberly like a judge: "In advocating any measure, I believe we must always consider not only its justice but its practicability. Regarding the laws relating to marriage, there should be the most *absolute equality* preserved between the two sexes. I do not think the woman should assume the man's name. And I would have the word 'obey' used not more by the wife than the husband."

Good for you, Theo. Good for you! These are beautiful, noble, exalted sentiments indeed … but practical? I wonder what Sunshine thinks about all this. And I wonder if Theo intends to put these lofty ideals into practice in his very own household—*and* marriage?

Perhaps I Will

WEDNESDAY

30 JUNE 1880

Today, Theo graduates from Harvard with a B.A. magna cum laude, Phi Beta Kappa, and a standing of twenty-one in his class of 177.

His adoring family will attend the graduation ceremony, of course.

I will not.

I wasn't invited. It's family only, you know.

Family now includes the large contingent from Chestnut Hill, including Alice Hathaway Lee.

During Theo's last visit home to see family, he confided to them (which Conie later divulged to me): "My cup of happiness is almost *too* full just now. Only four months before we get married!"

I think I'll see if Papa wants to accompany me to the theater tonight … it's *Fantinitza*, a Viennese operetta in an English translation, recently opened at the Edwin Booth Theater on Broadway. (I *love* that theater with its deep-red velour seats!)

Seeing a show is something to take my mind off things. I hope they'll still have some of the "cheap seats" available. True, you can scarcely see the actor's faces from way back there, but at least I can still *hear* them—as long as they talk loud enough.

THURSDAY

1 JULY 1880

Papa and I have a fine time last night at the theater, *despite* this particular production. It's a "mostly" English-language version of *Fantanitza*, a recently famous hit operetta in Vienna, but gosh-all-hemlock, it's hard to keep up with the plot. Here's why: the main character is the famous Viennese actress Antonie Link, who is most definitely a woman in *every* way … only, she is "playing" a *man* named Wladimir (pronounced with a V) … and this character, Wlad (or Vlad), is, at the same time, *supposed* to be a man … a *real* man … who is also, in the plot, "pretending to be a woman." Throughout the story, there are other men pretending to be women and women pretending to be men. It's confusing to say the least! At least the music is decent, but nothing special in my humble opinion.

When the show is over, Papa and I make a bee-line for the nearest exit and walk over to Luchow's, that marvelous German restaurant. I caution him before we go in, "Papa, remember we only have one dollar and seventy-five cents between us after the tickets." Papa emits a die-away sigh. He hates being poor, just *hates* it. "Don't worry," he finally dismisses my fears. "We'll split one order of cake with two coffees," which is what we do.

Our conversation over dessert is not about tonight's confusing, silly libretto. Instead, we have a spirited conversation about today's best-selling book that is *not Ragged Dick,* but none other than the *Five Little Peppers and How They Grew* by Margaret Sidney. The *Peppers* book is a secret favorite of mine that's more popular with school children, but adults nationwide now adore it, too. It's been said (and corroborated by the author) that her sequel, and any more *Pepper* books that come after this one, are going to be written specifically for adults.

Saturday

10 July 1880

There are no secrets between the families … Conie cheerfully reports "all things Roosevelt" whether I ask her to or not. That's how I know Alice recently took the train from Boston to Oyster Bay and then on to Tranquillity. Along with her handsome male cousin Dick Saltonstall and his homely-as-a-hedge-fence sister Rose, Alice will be staying there for a full four weeks. (That's one week longer than I was ever invited.)

Guess my pipe dream of—somehow—going out to Tranquillity in August isn't going to happen.

You ridiculous spinster—of course it isn't going to happen! Alice and Theo are engaged. You'd best remember that fact.

My inner self is all too quick to reprimand and berate me these days. As she should. Worry not, dear journal … it's only a critic in my brain; I'm not yet at the point of hearing audible voices. Thank goodness.

As I said, Conie writes me all the news, bidden or not.

However, secrets we dare not mention aloud to one another loom large in our lives and seem to multiply by the day. What secrets? Like the fact that boring Doug Robinson (who subconsciously squints and wrinkles his nose in unison) continues to pursue Conie against her wishes.

Doug is so dogged, determined, and teeth-jarringly dull. Conie can't stand, even, to hold his *hand,* let alone to think about performing more intimate attentions with this slope-shouldered bear of a man. This does not bode well for their future, be it separate or conjoined.

Plus, there's the equally embarrassing fact that Conie *finally* discerned—and simultaneously pities me, yet still feels a huffing annoyance over the fact—that I still carry an obvious "torch" for her brother. Because she knows I want to hear the news—good, bad, or indifferent—she continues to write me the "doings" of Theo and Alice. As boxing coaches are quoted as saying in the newspapers, Conie "pulls no punches."

In an earlier reply to one of Conie's letters, I cautiously asked my old friend, "And how do you find Alice's temperament? What does she like to read? Who are her favorite poets?"

Conie's return letter to me is blunt yet positive. "She's not like the rest of us. She doesn't *like t*o read books the way *we* do. But I can't help liking her. She *is* like her nickname—so cheerful, happy, and likable. Like … well … exactly what they call her: Sunshine."

Perhaps I Will

Sunday

25 July 1880

Just five days ago, Tuesday, 20 July 1880, the great obelisk, Cleopatra's Needle, *finally* arrived at its new, permanent location in Central Park! Such a great celebration there was and such cheering from the crowds that packed its route of travel. The final leg of the obelisk's journey was made by pushing it with a steam engine across a specially built trestle bridge from Fifth Avenue to its new home on Greywacke Knoll, just across the drive from the recently completed Metropolitan Museum of Art. (Oh, dear departed Greatheart—another of his noble accomplishments.) It took 112 days from the Quarantine Station to arrive at the knoll.

While Cleopatra's Needle was being maneuvered into place, T happened to be with Alice in Bar Harbor, Maine, with the Saltonstall cousins. At the very same time as the Cleopatra's Needle placement in Central Park, Theo came down with his old nemesis, cholera morebus: days of diarrhea, gas, cramps, and nausea.

Just a curious little coincidence, I guess. Theo frequently falls prey to this ... inconvenience ... when he's nervous or anxious. He wrote to Conie (who passed the details on to me): "Very embarrassing for a lover, isn't it! So unromantic, you know, suggestive of too much unripe fruit."

He took the words right out of my mouth.

Friday

30 July 1880

Johnny-on-the-spot Conie is all too quick to write and "remind" me that Alice's nineteenth birthday happened yesterday. They're still visiting in Maine—the four of them together, Alice and Theo, with Cousins Dick and Rose acting as chaperones.

The night of Alice's birthday, they all danced so much and so enthusiastically that Theo collapsed afterward—the dreaded cholera morebus yet *again.*

I wonder who is nursing Theo through the more ... um, unpleasant ... aspects of this malady? I'm thinking it's certainly not Queen Alice.

Friday

6 August 1880

I was wrong.

Conie now informs me that Alice "nursed" her affianced companion for several days of his sickness, "as solicitous as ever anyone could be!"

Their party of four has moved on to Tranquillity, where they meet up with Miss Mittie, Elliott, and Bamie. Theo will soon head west with Nell on a hunting trip, while Alice travels home to prepare for the wedding, happening in just a few short weeks.

Something else of note happens today: I too turn nineteen, as Alice did just a few days ago.

Alice is safely, happily engaged and (as the saying goes) "set for life."

I, on the other hand, am none of these things.

On a brighter note, I'm relieved to remind myself that I'm *still* officially a young lady of quality (well, marginally), if not exactly a belle of fashion (money is required for that). I remain still fresh enough to be considered appropriate marriage material—at least for one more year, anyway.

After that, I'll enter the dreaded decade, the twenties, when I shall magically turn into a spinster, an old maid.

That is, unless I convince some appropriate gentleman to marry me and convince myself to marry him. Soon…

Late August 1880

I don't need to write a specific date for this entry. It's all been happening over a series of days and then weeks. I'm finally writing it down now, higgledy-piggledy, whatever I've managed to glean from Conie's letters and random gossip.

About three weeks ago, Theo and Elliott left for their big hunting trip out west on the night train. Since then, they've been hunting in Illinois, Iowa, and northwestern Minnesota, with heaps of miles yet to go.

Although Theo's spirits are high, his physical ailments are apparently legion: cholera morebus (to the extent he can hardly walk sometimes) and also the dreaded asthma, so severe he sometimes has to sleep sitting up.

And there's more—both of the brothers' guns break, and T is bitten by a snake, thrown headfirst out of a wagon, soaked in rainstorms, and then battered by a freezing gale. Worst of all, dear Elliott—our own dear Nell—is starting to drink *far* too much. Theo is frightened by this state of affairs, has no idea what to do, and carefully starts informing the rest of the family about it in his letters.

As if Theo didn't have enough problems to worry about, what with the cholera morebus, persistent asthma, and marriage to Alice looming like an eastbound train on the tracks of his life.

Monday
30 August 1880

Conie and Bamie are home again from Tranquillity. It's so good to be with "the girls" again—even if Theo did ask Bamie to pack a suitcase for him with certain special items (mostly visiting clothes) and bid her to please have it ready for him when he returns.

I'm guessing that, when his train from the West pulls into Grand Central Station, he'll hop off—Theo always hops or jumps—and then rustle up a cab to take him home. There, he'll snatch up the suitcase Bamie packed to his specifications and immediately leap onto the train for Boston, where he'll hire a hansom cab and finally bask in the presence of Queen Alice.

Wednesday
1 September 1880

I received a surprise invitation recently from Fanny Smith herself—yes, she's still engaged to Commander Dana and shortly to be married in the U.S. Navy chapel in Annapolis, Maryland. We recently ran into one another at the stationery store, where she gave me a surprise hug and begged, "Come and gather autumn wildflower specimens with me, Edie! It's been everlastingly long since we've done anything like this, and we must get caught up before Theo's wedding. Let's go out to where they'll soon be opening the new Riverside Avenue—no one will mind if we take specimens from there because it'll be a muddy trampled roadway soon enough."

Fanny brought her plant press portfolio, and we collected more than twenty-seven specimens, including the root-balls as well. We both had a marvelous time and cared not at *all* that we both got mud along the hems of our skirts. It reminded me of old days with Theo, and I said as much to Fanny.

"Yes, and how funny to think we will both be getting married before the year is out!" Fanny looked bemused as she said this. I couldn't tell if the prospect of impending marriage was indeed "funny" to her or anything *but* that.

"Are you nervous?" I'm surprised that I asked her this, but I wanted to know.

After an awkward silence, she said, "Yes" and made a funny little face as she said it. "But we *have* to—who will look after us and feed us if we don't? It's a mortification to our parents, and especially to their friends, if we don't marry."

I was very surprised when she asked me, "Any prospects, Edie?"

I was so surprised that I answered her before thinking: "Nope." (Yes, I actually used the new slang word, improper as it is.)

"Well, all right then." And so *that* was *that*. Fanny kindly switched to a less-fraught topic: "Let's go down by the sailboat slips—I know I've seen milkweed growing there, and I could use some for my collection. You know I aim to write a wildflower guide before we start our family." Seeing my surprised look, Fanny rephrased that: "Someday, that is … someday."

In the evening *Times* today, it said that the man who invented margarine, Antoon Jurgens, died today. I wonder if death took him by surprise…

Perhaps I Will

Thursday

4 September 1880

I'm heading for the Newsboys' Lodging House to help out for dinner on Friday and Saturday. Plus, this morning I "worked on Papa" (and we know it doesn't take much) to see if we could get tickets for the new production of *Around the World in Eighty Days* at the Niblo's Garden Theater tonight. (Of course, he said yes, and I went into town to buy tickets ahead of time.) This new show has been on for a week so far, but I'll bet not very many people are sitting in the last row. I'm glad that we will be, Papa and I, and I'm not too proud to say it!

The happy wanderers—Theo and Nell—finally returned two days ago, happy with their haul of dead game animals, which were sent on ahead of their arrival. (Even now, the appropriate parts are being tended to by a local butcher and taxidermist, first one and then the other.)

As I'd suspected, Theo stopped in only long enough to grab up his prepacked valise of clothes before speeding on toward Boston. I didn't get a chance to tell him hello or goodbye, but then, I wasn't expecting to.

Alice was waiting for him, and (according to a letter from Conie, quoting her bedazzled big brother): "She looked lovelier than I'd ever seen her. I cannot take my eyes off her. She is so pure and holy that it seems almost a profanation to touch her, no matter how gently and tenderly, and yet when we are alone, I cannot bear her to be a minute out of my arms."

The words speak for themselves. Yes…

I don't seem to be able to rouse myself to make any comment about this. The more enraptured Theo feels with Alice, the more exhausted I feel.

Thursday

30 September 1880

Theo starts law school today at Columbia University, right here in Manhattan. Dear Theo is *finally* back home again in our very own city. But he seems to be taking particular pains *not* to run into me, on purpose or by accident—or in any other way altogether.

Monday

4 October 1880

On Saturday, 2 October, the Grand Master of Masons in the state of New York presided over an impressive Masonic ceremony to lay the cornerstone for the obelisk.

Over nine thousand Masons paraded up Fifth Avenue from 14th Street to 82nd Street. The newspapers estimated that more than fifty thousand spectators lined the parade route.

We three—Em, Mame, and I—were among them, adding our own ladylike cheers to the excited roar of the crowd.

I yearned to have Theo by my side to share my joy and pride in all the spectacle and "speech-ifying."

But only part of me—a small, whimpering part—was feeling like this.

The *rest* of me—sensible, resolute, pragmatic, and determined—was already hatching a plan.

SATURDAY

8 OCTOBER 1880

Today I head over to the Roosevelts' to pick up Conie before we visit the new traveling exhibit at the Metropolitan Museum of Art.

Miss Mittie is all a-twitter because Theo is due to show up in the city tonight, and as his mother explained (her forehead furrowed and expression pained): "Theo aims to spend a king's *ransom* of money—twenty-five *hundred* dollars!—on jewelry for Alice. Girls, you *know* I try not to worry about Dear Teedie, and he keeps reassuring me that he'll still be a loyal son

… but—oh, dear children, everything seems to be happening so *fast!*"

Then, Bamie takes her mother's two hands in hers … and stares her down.

"Worry not, Motherling. *This* time, Teedie's in *love*, and that makes everything all right!"

We all laugh at this, of course—well, *most* of us do. I refrain from laughter but I do (at least) show a glimmer of my Mona Lisa half-smile.

Miss Mittie exhales then. "You're right … of course you're right … I'm just being silly!"

Miss Mittie gained some "grief weight" since dear Greatheart died. She's starting to look like the middle-aged, plumpish mother she really is, instead of the belle of the ball.

With the Mona Lisa simper still on my face, Miss Mittie suddenly grabs *my* closest hand and squeezes it. "Oh, Edie! We are *so* grateful, dear, for the pre-wedding dinner you're hosting for Teedie. What a wonderful idea—a 'dinner for young persons only': family and school and neighborhood friends. We are all so appreciative of your kind and generous gesture ... especially, all things considered..."

Miss Mittie's stops talking then, evidently wishing she hadn't introduced the sensitive topic of the "torch" I continue to carry for her elder son.

She's not sure where to go with the rest of her sentence.

As part of my plan—to appear completely at ease with the way things are turning out—I broaden my Mona Lisa smile into a magnanimous, generous grin and attempt to set Miss Mittie at ease.

"Ah well, you know, ma'am ... we're *such* old friends, Teedie and I ... and why would I not wish him every happiness in his new, married life ahead?"

The words flutter out of my mouth with aplomb and conviction—I'd practiced ahead of time just what I'd say, if asked...

Even Mamma, Papa, Em, and Mame say very little to me in the way of opposition when I tell my family—yes, I told them about it as a *fait accompli;* I did *not* "ask permission"—I'd be spending a shocking amount of our household budget on a catered formal dinner in Theo's honor.

(Not hers … not in Alice's honor … only *his* honor. His and his alone.)

For some time now, I've been budgeting, scrimping, unobtrusively selling odds and ends to the used furniture dealer and saving for this event, even when it was still a vague mirage in my mind.

Then, I told the Roosevelt women what I'd like to do. And they told Theo.

The women were pleased as punch. Theo seemed embarrassed, but then he said yes and thanked me effusively in advance.

I'm hiring Delmonico's to deliver the meal—partridges, two modest joints of beef, jellied quail eggs with many fixings, and the popular Nesselrode pie for dessert—service for twenty "young people," including Em, who is secretly thrilled to be included.

Mame and I will put both leaves into our dining room table so it's extra-long. Delmonico's will serve the meal elegantly with two hired, liveried footmen and one extra serving maid (to help Mame) for the evening. I figure Em and I can help Mame with the washing-up afterward, long after the guests have gone home.

Mamma says very little when I tell her what I'm going to do—*surely* she must know how this Roosevelt situation is a painful crisis for me. All of her old anger and horror over the Roosevelt's "scrofula situation" seems to have dissipated into the ether.

Mamma seems so subdued these days. Can she actually be worrying about me? About my heart? About my precarious situation as a would-be old maid?

Poor, dear Papa says nothing at all. He merely gives a hesitant half-smile when I tell him about the dinner. His chin quivers, and he replies, "What a generous gesture, Daughter. How like you to be *so* kind to such an old friend. *Especially* when…"

Perhaps I Will

Papa stops talking then.

When I tell Em about it, she rolls her eyes at me, but even Em doesn't carp or complain for a change. I suppose she figures that a fancy dinner like this ... something different, elegant, and exciting in our simple lives ... is something to be savored and enjoyed, no matter what the cost.

Even if Em's big sister happens *not* to be the bride.

Only fourteen days until the wedding.

I keep up the ridiculous hope that maybe there'll be an earthquake, flood, an invasion—or *something*, *anything* to keep this wedding from taking place.

Wednesday

13 October 1880

No flood, so far. No earthquake. No invasion.

Nothing to hold back the relentless approach of the dreaded wedding.

Have it your own way, destiny. So be it, then.

I keep nodding and smiling; like Macbeth, I screw my courage to the sticking spot and press forward toward my own date with destiny.

My elegant "little party for young people" in honor of Theo turns out to be a rousing—and surprisingly satisfying—success, with constant laughter and jokes, along with tributes and toasts to the man of the hour.

(Even as I smile, I keep thinking *this surely cannot be ... this surely cannot be real ...* but, oh yes, it was and still *is*. Every minute we move closer toward the wedding date.)

Even *I* can't help but enjoy myself at the dinner because Theo seems so unutterably happy. He's irrepressible when he's happy—everyone around him *must* be happy too, and they succumb to his charms helplessly. There's no escaping Theo's infectious joy, even as I mentally roll my eyes and look down on my spinster self with distant pity.

Theo even does his usual stunt of tipping Fanny Smith's chair back so precipitously that she emits an uneasy giggle that ends in a squawk.

(Theo "catches" the chair at the last moment, of course. It's something he always does with her because he likes to get a rousing scream out of her polite, well-bred self. She continues to adore him from afar even though she's engaged to Commander Dana—it's undeniable.)

Fanny wrote me a "bread-and-butter" letter after the party, wherein she shared, "Teedie is as funny as ever, isn't he! Funny, delicious, and wild with happiness and excitement. I went with him the following day to see the wedding presents he plans to give Alice. I *do* hope she is very fond of him. Just think—only one more week 'til the wedding!"

Her comment about Alice being "fond" surprised—jarred—me a bit. Perhaps I'm not the only female with unvoiced reservations about the likelihood of happiness in their marriage?

Even when invited by the Roosevelt girls, I politely opted *not* to "go and see the presents."

After all, I can only smile so much, and my smiles are stretched perilously thin these days.

SUNDAY

17 OCTOBER 1880

The morning *Times* reports today that the earliest, strongest, major blizzard in "man's memory" covered Dakota Territory with several feet of snow. It's not even Halloween yet!

The paper is saying that some of the older Native peoples—among the few who are still left in that country—are foretelling an unbelievably long, hard winter ahead. I'm so glad that Theo and Elliott returned from their western hunting trip when they did.

MONDAY NIGHT

25 OCTOBER 1880

Fanny has gone off to the lobby here at the hotel in Brookline to see if Grace has arrived yet. *Good ...* that'll give me a couple minutes to be alone with my journal.

I feel I must record my feelings ... but for what? Or whom? For posterity? (Who will care in another hundred years? Or even another day?)

Perhaps I Will

Even so, I am still drawn to record the details, like a convicted prisoner facing the guillotine. The blade will fall in just two days.

Do I feel that Theo and Alice's wedding will bring the end of my life?

No, not really. Life as I know it? Yes, it'll be the end of *that*, of course.

But the wedding will also presage the start of a new life for me—a life that I must start immediately, with resolve, endurance, fortitude, and determination.

(Yes, I know I keep *saying* this, but I have to start *doing* this!)

If I can't live my life with Theo, then I resolve to make another life of worth, value, and meaning—be it with another worthy gentleman or as an industrious spinster, sowing good wherever I can.

Fanny Smith and I arrive in Boston today, 25 October, two days before the wedding. Four of us girls—Grace Potter, Fanny Smith, Annie Murray, and I—reserved ahead of time to share a single room with two double beds. Then Annie

Murray came down with "la grippe" and had to stay home. Somehow I managed (politely, I hope) to dibs one bed all for myself, and Fanny readily agreed to share the second bed with Grace.

I want a bed all to myself tonight in case I wish to hide evidence of surreptitious, unbidden tears.

Just because I'll soon be starting a new life of meaning, value, and goodness, it doesn't mean I'm looking forward to the prospect.

Anything but.

Tuesday

26 October 1880

Today—the day before the big W—the rest of the wedding guests, invited friends, and family invade the hotel, trilling happy wedding greetings punctuated with laughter to one and all.

The wedding guests are too numerous to track. This morning, group after group sets out in hired carriages to explore the city of Boston. Tonight, most of the immediate wedding party—not me, of course, although I'm not far away at a lesser table in the corner—will dine together at the long table already set up in the elegant dining room.

LATER tonight:

Theo's wedding ushers—his cousins Jimmy and Emlin—join the throng at dinner. What a breath of fresh air these lads are! They are so wisecracking and fun. I almost forget the impending doom that awaits tomorrow.

The bride-to-be, flanked and protected by the entire Lee clan, will make her appearance tomorrow … when the groom first glimpses her at the altar, where she'll stand quivering, clutching her father's arm.

Amid the noise, toasts, and well-wishing, I hear Theo say something that will stay with me always: "My happiness is so great now that it makes me almost afraid."

Did he have a premonition, I wonder?

*Did he suspect what destiny had in store for him—for **them**?*

I will always wonder—and won't know for sure until I "go on ahead myself."

Wedding Day Wednesday
27 October 1880

Today is Theo's twenty-second birthday—and the start of his new life with his new wife-to-be, Alice Hathaway Lee. I happened to hear Theo in the corridor on his way down to breakfast, talking with Elliott; they didn't notice I was within earshot. "Today is the day of my birth. And my birth of new happiness!"

Nearby in the dining room, I don't linger over my tea and toast. Instead, I hurry upstairs to change into my wedding garb.

(I mean my wedding *guest* garb: dimity white gown, not too low-necked because it's a daytime wedding, and dotted with small blue and white blossoms. My old short-heeled satin dancing slippers will have to do; nobody looks much at shoes anyway when a gown is sufficiently becoming.)

The next time I write in this journal—floods, invasions, or earthquakes notwithstanding—I shall do so as a new person, writing a new chapter in my book of life. I will be a person with no longer *any chance* of ever becoming Mrs. Theodore Roosevelt II. More about this later…

LATER tonight:

I'm writing the details of the wedding in the present tense because that is how I'm still experiencing them and feel them *still* that way within my heart: present tense in the eternal now.

Riding together, Fanny Smith and I are conveyed via hansom cab to the Unitarian Church in Brookline, about six miles out of Boston; Grace shares another cab with another former classmate from Miss Comstock's.

It's to be a simple, unpretentious, daytime wedding. Destiny is only too happy to do it up right: sunny, warm, and beautiful, not a cloud in the sky. It feels more like mid-June than late October.

Men take off their suit coats and hats.

Then it's time to start assembling in the church. Without actually running (but moving swiftly nonetheless), I somehow manage to snag a seat on the center aisle about halfway back on the left.

I'm afraid I've made a mistake—it's officially the "bride's side" of the church. But I don't care. I want a good seat.

Fanny and Grace sit beside me, glad to have a good-enough view. I don't slide over and give up my aisle position—I want an unencumbered view.

I just want to … see. And make sure it's really happening.

(No earthquake, flood, or invasion just yet. I'd say the likelihood is lower than zero.)

Bridesmaids slowly march in to dulcet tones of a string quartet playing Canon in D by Pachelbel.

Perhaps I Will

Theo and his groomsmen step from an anteroom to assemble at the altar, awaiting the bride.

Then, loud no-nonsense chords of the Lohengrin processional stir the guests to stand as the bride glides in on her father's arm. Too helpless to resist this strong emotion, we're all carried along on the all-powerful current of the Roosevelt-Lee wedding at last—a loving, relentless undertow that holds us all in its thrall.

Before I know it, he is actually saying those words:

"I, Theodore, do take you, Alice…"

(Ah, such resolute, Theodore-like tones.)

They are shortly echoed by a sweet, breathy voice: "I, Alice, take you, Theodore, to be my lawfully wedded husband."

(I wonder for a moment why they do not say "thee" instead of you; I surmise that the Unitarian church must be more contemporary than the High-Church Trinity Episcopal that the Carows attend in Manhattan.)

But don't say it, please don't say it … it *can't* be time to say it *yet* … where is the flood, invasion, or earthquake?

Words from an old Asian quote—Ancient History, courtesy of Miss Comstock herself—drift through my mind: "The current of life is ever onward."

I now hear the words that change everything for me—and for Theo and Alice, too: "I now pronounce you man and wife."

Helpless to do otherwise, I find my eyelids sliding shut. I can't help silently repeating the ancient intonation: *ashes to ashes, dust to dust…*

It is done.

They are well and truly married now, even as the minister drones on—I don't hear his homily anymore.

The old Edie Carow is now dead. I vow to arise now and *live* as Edith Kermit Carow, an independent young woman of purpose, fortitude, and new beginnings.

And for heaven's sake—my inner critic admonishes me—*no nonsense this time. Go out there and dance, really* dance, *at this wedding. Smile, flirt, and dance until the soles fall off your shoes! After all, it's the first day of the rest of your life.*

Chords of the recessional blare suddenly from the organ in the choir loft above.

I open my eyes, just in time to see the bride and groom—arm in arm—rustling slowly toward me down the aisle.

Theo doesn't see me there as they pass, but Alice does.

She looks at me warily.

I return her a Mona Lisa smile with a barely perceptible nod. I think she sees me, but I'm not sure.

The afternoon reception at the Lee mansion on Chestnut Hill is replete with sunshine, laughter, and flowing champagne. The reception is a glorious success.

When the afternoon waltzes and German polkas commence, I find myself tingling with a strange new energy. I find myself flirting—yes, actually flirting!—with every man who crosses my path, available or otherwise.

Yes. I fulfill my promise to destiny, and in the process (if I do say so myself), I do more dancing than any other girl at the reception—even the bride.

It actually feels so *good*—such an exhilarating feeling.

Around 4 p.m., the bride and groom bid their guests farewell. They're heading off to Springfield, Massachusetts, where Theo reserved a suite of rooms for one night at the old Massasoit House. Then, they're continuing on to Tranquillity to spend their autumn honeymoon in quiet and privacy (except for the servants, of course).

I make it a special point *not* to wave the bridal pair off and predictably pelt them with uncooked rice and warm wishes. Out of the corner of my eye, I see them leave while I'm deep in conversation with a young Massachusetts man named Gerard Osterman.

Later tonight, I'm foolishly pleased to discover that the flimsy soles of my aging dancing slippers have, indeed, become dislodged; I've danced the soles off my shoes just as I vowed. I made the acquaintance of several likely, eligible men … also as I vowed.

However, later on—in the darkest of darks, in my heart of hearts—I couldn't help thinking of Theo and Alice. It is night now, their wedding night. They're sharing what *I* always wanted to share … Theo and me, alone.

It's well after midnight. For the first time ever, I need some Dutch courage.

Still fully dressed, except for my shoes, I pad softly downstairs to the open door of the hotel's commodious smoking room. Unobtrusive servants clean and tidy the room, while a few clusters of gentlemen laugh and smoke cigars together, sharing pleasantries over wine or spirits. I spy the open archway to a butler's pantry nearby—just a couple steps should do it without any notice by the gentlemen. Silently, I tiptoe to the room where spirits are kept.

Several half-full bottles of wine remain on a drainboard, along with an open box of tissue-wrapped claret glasses.

Surreptitiously, I unwrap one of the small glasses. I pour myself some red wine—how much or what kind, I couldn't tell you. I drink the glass fully without stopping, as I would for a medicinal potion, and then I make my way back on silent feet to my communal room. Fanny and Grace are still snoring gently with happy, post-wedding exhaustion.

The wine burned a little as I chugged it down, but then it soon warmed me. I hoped it would help remind me of my new assemblage of possible suitors and then, finally, allow me to *sleep* … and to blot out any thoughts of Theo and Alice in the same bed, together, in the dark.

So far, the wine isn't working.

Friday night

12 November 1880

Today, the long-awaited book, *Ben-Hur* by Civil War General Lew Wallace, is hot off the presses.

Perhaps I Will

The *Times* reports this morning that folks are already lined up at bookstores to buy it before the shops were even open. Critics are already saying this "Christian dramatic adventure story within a spiritual framework" is going to sell like hotcakes! I know that Conie intends to buy a copy, so I'll wait and borrow hers after she reads it. It's been said that the tall, lean, dramatic-looking general who wrote this Biblical tale did his best work while sitting under the shade of the Portico at the ancient Palace of the Governors in far-away New Mexico Territory … day after day, month after month, while awaiting new orders from the military. That's why the book grew to be so long. I heard that *Ben-Hur* ended up with 442 pages of extremely small print. (Not at all like the *Five Little Peppers!*)

And on to other news … tomorrow, freshly returned from their honeymoon, Mr. and Mrs. Theodore Roosevelt II will take up official residence just nine blocks away from my house.

Yes, they're making their new home in the Roosevelt mansion, the one the family always calls "West Fifty-Seventh" (6 West 57th Street).

I have this on good authority from the Roosevelt sisters, who can't wait for their beloved brother to bring his new bride into their midst.

"The children" don't need to buy a home of their own just yet; Miss Mittie has plenty enough room for them all. She loves to have her children gathered about her—well, *most* of them, most of the time … Theo, Elliott, and Conie, specifically.

As for Bamie, she and her mother are currently (and noisily) "being contentious." The older they become, the more noisome each becomes. Still and all though, they're family. While her languid, semi-helpless widowed mother lives on, Bamie—so outgoing and officious—wouldn't dream of living anywhere else. She adores managing a large, bustling household and won't give it up for anything.

Theo and Alice will move into their own suite of rooms, though, including Alice's "own private parlor for receiving her own guests"— *and* on her own terms and inclination. Conie says Alice plans to hold Tuesday afternoon tea parties. (I hope she won't invite me. She probably won't.)

Alice already signed up—in advance—for the fashionable Drina Potter's Tennis School. Miss Potter had better look out! Theo says (admiringly, of course) that Alice has a "truly wicked serve."

Suddenly, I feel very tired, inadequate, and somehow abashed, as if Alice will make more of a mark on Manhattan in her first nineteen days than I have in my last nineteen years.

Sunday night

14 November 1880

No, I still haven't seen nor talked to the married Alice myself yet in person.

I expect I shall soon, though. I've "girded my loins" and won't shrink back. I'm ready.

But I *did* so want to see Theo first. I hear in passing from Bamie that Theo plans to "do dinner" on Sunday, tonight, at the Newsboys'

Lodging House, just the way his father used to do, every Sunday in the gathering darkness, sitting at the head of the long table, boys seated on both sides and hanging on his every word.

I made sure that *I'd* be helping out at the Newsboys' Lodging House this evening too. After sending the House a note via messenger boy—saying I'd be "coming in to help tonight with the serving"—I decided I'd slice mounds of bread and butter them, arranging them in haphazard heaps on plates, and set them out at intervals along the long table.

So finally, here I am, my kitchen work done. I watch Theo from afar from the kitchen doorway.

There he is, as promised—sitting at his father's former place at the table.

I can't help but smile—again, as ever, in my futile love of him—as he talks to his "lads," praising, inquiring, quietly admonishing, and enthusiastically instructing. They lap it up like cream.

How could I ever intentionally avoid that voice, that young man who so cheerfully

Perhaps I Will

yet decisively "bites his words" … who still mesmerizes me utterly?

As dinner concludes and each newsboy carries his own dirty dishes toward the kitchen, Theo finally notices me, peering out at him from behind the ajar green baize door.

He smiles and then gestures to me to come closer, no doubt to share a few words. My diaphragm is quivering as I comply.

I'm hardly at my best. Despite my overt flirting and non-stop dancing at Theo's wedding reception, I've found that flirting doesn't come naturally to me. It feels so forced, almost dishonest somehow. Plus, it's very hard work. (Especially when I feel less than nothing for the man I'm flirting with.)

Another thing—I find myself starting to dress more soberly now. I can't help it; it just happens. Anyway, the morality of society won't let me "dress up" for Theo. For one thing, it would be an affront to Alice, and for another, it would be an embarrassment to Theo. So I'm "dressing plain" these days in simple garb, including what I'm wearing tonight: an unadorned, very dark blue gown with a single line of black buttons down the bodice.

As befitting a respectable, nearly twenty-year-old spinster.

And Theo?

Oh, Theo looks wonderful.

He's glowing, even—infused, as ever, with life and vitality. Marriage obviously agrees with him.

After we share a few smiling but awkward pleasantries together, he bids me goodbye, shakes my hand—*shakes my hand*—and exits the premises. After all, Alice is waiting for him at home.

After doing a sufficient share of clean-up with a couple of other spinsters (much older than I), I bid them a friendly farewell: "Thank you and good evening, ladies!"

Then, I turn to Mrs. Abbott, the weekend cook, and say, "Well, um, goodbye then, Mrs. Abbott, and thank you."

She pivots from the sink to look at me in surprise. Obviously, she'd forgotten I was still there.

Cheerful but distracted, Mrs. Abbott chirps back, "Goodbye, Miss Carow. See you back again shortly."

Shortly … yes. Undoubtedly, I'll be back again soon.

There is so much dirt, death, and misery in the underbelly of Manhattan. So many good deeds that need doing to help carry the burden of others, whether my heart is breaking or not.

"Yes," I say to Mrs. Abbott's back, as she returns to the pot she is scrubbing. "Yes, I'll be back again. Soon."

The following day, Monday 15 November 1880

No time to brood over Theo now because Conie's nerves are all awhirl over an escalation of her existing romantic crisis.

At the Roosevelt house, we even invite a couple of my former classmates over to see what can be done about "the problem of Conie."

Fanny Smith, Annie Murray, and I stare at Conie, who sits across from us at the round tea table in the sun parlor.

Conie looks troubled and defeated, like a flustered witness for the defense who has no idea how to refute the charges piling against her.

"Girls … I mean, ladies … Mother and Bamie, even Theo—and *Alice*, for goodness' sake! … they *all* keep badgering and *badgering* me to … well, to accept old, grumpy-faced Robinson's ring!"

Annie, Fanny, and I look at one another—*that* doesn't sound *too* terribly bad. Does it?

Fanny Smith speaks first. "Would that *really* be so bad, dear heart? See what *I* have gone and done at the express request of Commander Dana…" She displays her left hand on the tablecloth for all to see.

A ring set with a garnet, flanked by two tiny, twinkling diamonds, glows in the late afternoon lamplight. A chorus of oohs and ahhs greets Fanny's admission of guilt.

I'm suddenly, silently furious. *Enough, Fanny.*

I *know* that Fanny remains head over heels for Theo, even as I am. She always has been. And she's always been much "nicer" to him than I—always gushing and cooing (earnestly and honestly) over everything he says or does ... instead of calling him out on things when it's called for. (As we all know, Theo isn't exactly one hundred percent right on *everything*. Not *hardly!*)

But, like the Roosevelt sisters, Fanny always chooses to overlook things ... she never needles him about questionable decisions and ill-timed remarks. I just can't help it, even as my love for him keeps growing deeper, stronger, and more pervasive. Go figure.

"Yes, my own wedding to Naval Commander Will Dana is now set for the first week of December. We'll be married at the Naval Academy Chapel in Annapolis," our lovely, dark-haired friend explains, with a slight, sheepish roll of her eyes. "Yes, yes he *is* sixteen years older than I am. But still, it feels right. *He* feels right, somehow."

I don't know if that's a compliment to Fanny or not, so I say nothing. But the gears and wheels of my mind are clicking and clacking about furiously, like mechanical squirrels. I'm thinking: *Theo and Fanny ... she's always,* always *adored him, even as I have. But now—is she being pragmatic and contentedly "resigned?" Sensibly accepting her second-choice candidate because her number one man has married someone else?*

I'm thinking *that's it*, and more power to her. She's a better woman than I am to pull off this painful and difficult feat.

Then, I admit to myself that a girl on the verge of spinsterhood, even a "financially modest yet comfortable" girl like Miss Frances Theodora Smith, must weigh her options carefully. A respectable husband "in the hand" has *got* to be worth more than a wayward lover "in the bush." Right?

I think *yes*—so long as she has the fortitude and determination to stick it out and see it through, like Charlotte Lucas in *Pride and Prejudice* who marries Mr. Collins for "practical reasons." Strong, annoying, yet spiritual Fanny has those sensible qualities "in spades," as the coarse vernacular goes.

We four girls erupt into conversation around the table.

All of this talk and adrenaline rouses me to become animated and involved. No one would guess that I'm still pining for a man I cannot have.

Finally … *finally* … we hound, nag, plead, and eventually convince Conie to "just *take* his ring and tell him *yes,* because, well, dear … what other choice do you have? He's rich and not stingy—yes, we agree he's often annoying and irascible, *but* he usually lets you have your own way. And, besides, it's *time. No* other suitors await in the wings of your theater."

We convince Conie that her mother will *never* let up on her—true—and she'll likely never find a candidate as respectable and wealthy as Douglas Robinson, no matter how long she looks. Or waits.

Limp yet surly with defeat, Conie growls softly in her own defense: "I don't *love* him, you know…"

Sanctimonious, goody-two-shoes Annie Murray pats Conie's clasped hands. "You can *learn* to love him, dear girl. It'll come out all right … in the end."

"Easy for *you* to say." Finally, Conie capitulates. "All right, I'll do it."

Her words are punctuated with a die-away sigh. "I can't fight you all—and Mother, too."

Annie and Fanny smother Conie with hugs. I finally get my chance to—what?—show my support, I guess, as well.

I lean in, put my arm around her waist, pull her close, and whisper in her right ear: "It'll be all right … you'll see … and, as they say, 'needs must.'"

She looks at me then, accusingly. She must know. She *has* to know that I still yearn after Theo. But she knows I can do nothing about it—

any more than she can outrun Doug Robinson. Or Miss Mittie.

She gives me a reluctant squeeze back, looks glaze-eyed into the inner distance, and repeats, "You're right ... you're right ... needs must."

Then—wouldn't you just know—Annie Murray simpers and announces to the group, "See what misery *you're* escaping, Edie? All because of your 'utter lack of susceptibility' to eligible men?"

All of us laugh then—even me. A little.

Utter lack of susceptibility, eh?

In the space of a heartbeat, I take stock of my future as it stands now.

Theo and Alice have a life together and a future.

Eventually, too, will Fanny Smith, as she and her not-so-young Naval Commander William Dana create a new life together.

Even Annie Murray exchanges bad poetry with her cousin Fred's Princeton roommate.

And Conie and Doug will surely make *some* kind of life together.

Won't they?

Only *I* appear—to them—to have an "utter lack of susceptibility" to all men. But I vow to start changing my vibrations and intentions. I *must*.

I *have* to find a likely second best with whom to make a family, a marriage, and a life, lest my existence dwindles down into a dim, shadowy half-life of only doing good deeds and reading (and re-reading) the Bible, Shakespeare, Blake, Coleridge, Southey, Dickens, Thackeray—oh yes, and Henry James.

I'm merely existing.

Not truly living.

Wednesday

17 November 1880

Conie capitulated in life and love— according to Elliott, who, from his tiger hunt in India, writes unhappy letters back to Miss Mittie and Bamie saying Conie's decision is all a "terrible mistake."

Maybe it is.

We'll never know until later, when it's too late to do anything about it.

Conie's marriage to Doug wasn't a "terrible mistake," but it was an accommodation only— "something to do" while she waited in vain for a Prince Charming of her own. A Prince Charming who never arrived. At least in the meanwhile, Doug Robinson gave her children and a respectable place in society, even if he never won her heart.

It feels a relief to me that Conie no longer struggles and writhes against the direction of her life. Although she won't be any happier for accepting Doug—just the opposite, most likely—at least it'll be easier for Conie to flow with the current. Just like I am flowing along on my *own* current, for better or for worse.

I think society at large simply wore Conie out. (Yes, we girls don't help matters any.) A knight in shining armor hasn't shown up yet for Conie and probably never will. There's only Doug Robinson, the loyal but irascible Scotsman, wealthy in his own right and manager-advisor of the vast Astor properties.

Conie gave her official "yes" to Doug two days ago; she now (half-heartedly) flashes an impressive engagement ring whenever she moves her left hand.

Conie also agrees—listlessly—to Miss Mittie's grand plans for a coming-out party, even though Conie no longer *needs* to "come out" because she's already officially engaged. But Miss Mittie wants a party, and she shall have one. Invitations just went out to more than six hundred, inviting them to a gala reception in honor of her daughter Corinne at the Roosevelt mansion on 8 December 1880.

Conie even leaves the design and style of her debut gown fully to her mother, asking only that she be allowed sole decision and selection of the flowers to adorn her dress and hair.

"Daisies, I want daisies," is Conie's mulish request, even though hot-house daisies aren't all that easy to come by in December. But enough money can buy you most anything these days, and she shall have her daisies. (In a worried, indiscreet moment, Bamie confided to me that her mother is "going through their money" at a furious rate, and Conie's marriage to wealthy Doug is more of a necessity than anyone wants to admit.)

Conie also divulges to me what her mother said about Doug, "and, Edie, she actually *said* this to me, which cut me to the quick! She said: 'I think you will be able to stand him, even though he's kind of dour. He's a very fine man, but very, very plain. But it's not a bad plainness. It's like quinine. It's a clean plainness.' I ask you … a 'clean plainness'—*is* there even such a thing!? At least he has a good 'strong and tender' side, much like Father."

When we're able to talk privately, Conie continues to confess—how shall I say it?—her anxiety about the personal side of marriage.

As it happens, Doug's younger sister feels that way, too, about her own fiancé. Both girls are engaged to marry men they don't know very well. As Conie explains, "She and I *both* say we would like to be suddenly married already, for about a year, for example, without knowing anything about it, and then things wouldn't look so frightening."

After a gulp and a sidelong glance, Conie adds, "Perhaps it was not *meant* for me to marry, or I wouldn't have this horror of it. Sometimes I think if I could just talk to Father, things would be all right."

Another letter from Elliott shows up, begging the family to allow Conie to break off the engagement because "it would be misery for both of them to enter into a marriage in which the wife felt no love."

It's too late now. That train has already left the station. Already, it gains momentum as it roars down the tracks. The wedding date is set for 29 April 1882.

Monday

22 November 1880

I *have* to get Conie out of the house tonight! Literally and figuratively.

This afternoon, I beg and wheedle with her: "*Please?* Come with me tonight to see Lillian Russell make her debut at Tony Pastor's on Broadway! It's opening night. I'll get us good seats ahead of time if you'll chip in. *Come* on, Con, you *must* … it'll do you a world of good to get out and about! You know Lillian Russell is playing D'Jenna in *The Snake Charmer,* right? and her 'fella' Diamond Jim Brady will be there, too?—they're better than the actual show!"

Finally, she comes around. (I think she is secretly glad to do so.)

So off we go. We've got *excellent* seats, thanks to Conie's abundant pocket money.

The show is *great* fun, *so* alluring and more than a little titillating, but nothing we couldn't tell our mothers about afterward. Lillian Russell is so *young!* (Exactly my age, but she looks even younger—I asked the chatty ticket agent about her age, and nineteen *is* still very young, unless you're thinking about marriage prospects, and if that is the case, then I'm already almost too old, but I digress...)

Lillian Russell has the *most* "hour-glassy" figure of *any* hourglass figure I've ever seen! She has such a tiny perfect waist, generous hips and bosoms, long, thick, wavy, brown hair, and pale, crystal-blue eyes, almost like Alice's—well, that part is a little unnerving. (I told you we had excellent seats, close enough to see the color of her eyes.)

In her character as D'Jenna, the Snake Charmer, Miss Russell plays fearlessly with live snakes on stage. She looks simultaneously shocking yet glorious in her shin-length dress with the very short sleeves, her slender body wound around and around with an extra-long, form-fitting stole with Greek-looking circular symbols.

The show is like a cheerful tonic to Conie—to us *both!* I don't have to ask Conie twice about "waiting around after the show to see if

Diamond Jim Brady will show up." Along with about half the audience, Conie and I wait, too.

Soon, there she is … Lillian Russell herself, shaking the gloved hands of fawning society belles and mustache-twirling men of money. Conie and I hang back, happy to enjoy the spectacle without being a part of it.

Finally, there *he* was, Diamond Jim Brady himself, sliding one arm around Lillian Russell's slim waist in a possessive manner. He's not handsome at *all*—dear Lord, he must weigh 300 pounds! Or *more*—but *so suave* is he, with an irresistible voice that make goosebumps shimmer down my backside.

Someone in the crowd calls out to him in a strong Irish accent but still in a good-natured way: "So are you hungry then, Mr. Brady?"

He pulls Lillian around to face him. He squeezes her, looks into her eyes, and grins, "You bet I am!"

"And what are you hungry *for*, Mr. Brady?" the Irish voice teases again.

Everyone expects him to say something lascivious or coarse about being hungry for her, um, charms. But he only smiles at Miss Russell more broadly and says: "I'm hungry for what's on the menu at Rector's tonight ... my favorite eatery, y'know ... so because it's Monday night, that'll probably be two or three deviled crabs, a brace of boiled lobsters, a joint of beef, and an enormous salad, topped off by several pieces of homemade pie and some orange juice. And the same for Miss Russell—I'm teaching dear Lillian to eat the same way *I* do!"

Everyone laughs uproariously at them both—the slim, gorgeous young girl and the middle-aged fat man with a diamond stick pin, collar studs, and cuff links.

Wednesday

8 December 1880

I'm being officially "courted" tonight by a man named Jack Trayner Stratton. When it rains, it sometimes pours, for I have three *more* dates coming up soon, waiting in the wings: Edgar Mulder, Elrod Blake, and Percy Mayes.

Jack is an old family friend of Doug Robinson's. Conie says I simply *must* have a gentleman caller escort me to her debut party, and Jack will be perfect in so many ways. "Shall I set it up for you?"

I throw caution to the wind, shrug, said why not and fine, and, soon after, I ask: "Who *is* this fellow Jack, anyway?

Conie replies that he's from a financially comfortable family who's in the millwork lumber business. (That tells me the *what* but not the *who.*)

Not long after I accept Jack's invitation to Conie's party, three *more* gentleman callers appeared on my horizon, all within the same week—young, single men I'd danced and flirted with at Theo's wedding. They presented their cards at my door, along with polite invitations to accompany me to the theater (Edgar), a "musicale night" at a railroad magnate's mansion

(Elrod), and a charity afternoon dance on behalf of the Little Italians tutoring program for children of immigrants (Percy).

I'll write more tonight before I fall into bed—in the wee hours of the morning, I imagine—after Conie's big night.

My other assignations—courting dates—are coming up within the next couple of weeks as well. I'll tell you all about them and hold nothing back. How *satisfying* it is to have someone ... some *thing* ... *you,* dear Woman's Journal ... to confide in and know you'll never argue back against me—or tattle about—my motives, hopes, fears, and dreams!

More later...

MUCH, MUCH LATER

Jack Trayner Stratton was nothing like I'd dreaded he might be. He's actually quite handsome (except for his eyes, which don't exactly "match"). He's very pleasant, too. He asked me to go out with him again, and I said yes, I'd love to go. He's taking me for an afternoon of skating at the new "artificial" ice rink at Madison Square Garden—nobody can quite figure out how they make artificial ice! It either *is ice* or it *isn't?* Right?

So how does one describe the external attributes of Jack Stratton? First, he's of average height—yes, much like Theo—slim and trim (the word "neat" comes to mind). His head is narrow (El Greco) and his hair close-cropped and brunette. A narrow, too-thin-for-fashion mustache, aquiline nose and very nice lips (if I do say so myself) complete his pleasing face.

Most girls would call Jack *very* good-looking, and, for the most part, he is … except for his eyes, which are too close together and make me uncomfortable to look at. His eyes aren't twinkling, blue, and deep like Theo's. I'd call them "flat ovals" instead—no, make that almond shapes, the color of coffee beans under slanting, black brows. An interesting face, yes, but more "disconcerting" than handsome. "Vulpine" describes it better.

But back to Conie's coming-out party tonight…

It's been a long time since I've hobnobbed with New York's rich and famous (not that I ever have much—we're not enough well-fixed for that). But tonight, at Conie's party, I hobnob with them and with an escort, too—a true, genteel gentleman.

I notice that *I* got noticed more, too—more than usual—with an interesting young man carefully "guiding my elbow" most everywhere I went.

I have to say that, yes, it is interesting, mixing and chatting with New York City's finest four hundred and other assorted guests (more than six hundred people in all, not counting permanent and rented staff for the night).

I feel oddly elevated and empowered above the fray (then feel ashamed of myself for doing so), especially when Conie continues to mist-over with tears, over and over again.

Miss Mittie is *so* embarrassed by Conie and her sinking spells. She keeps trying to change the subject and/or pinch Conie's arm to make her stop, but it doesn't work. None of the guests

Perhaps I Will

say anything, though. They just keep drinking and dancing.

Even dear Aunt Annie Gracie comes out of her sickbed to attend the party—"I wouldn't miss this for the world!"—but the house is so hot, "close," and jammed with bodies, she finally retreats back upstairs to lie down.

Jack and I even convey our greetings to Mrs. William Astor herself—yes, *the* Mrs. Astor, New York's queen (and arbiter) of high society. This very grand dame's late husband had vast holdings and properties—now hers—that are managed by none other than the groom-to-be, Doug Robinson.

The nouveau riche are here at the party, too, in force. They are dressed to the nines, of course, braying loudly and drinking conspicuously throughout the night: Vanderbilts, Dodges, Harrimans, Iselins, and so many more. The Old Knickerbocker Guard is there—Rutherfurds, Coopers, Schermerhorns, and so many more I can't keep them all straight. Even the king arbiter of society himself, Ward McAllister, is there. These luminaries venture out into the freezing winds and blowing sleet tonight to grace the brightly lit Roosevelt mansion at West 57th. These bodies now generate a fierce amount of heat. Hostess/facilitator Bamie goes from window to window on the main floor, flinging them open to the winter storm. The cold air pouring in feels *wonderful.*

Conie's gown of muslin and Valenciennes lace is graced with a corsage of—what else?—*daisies*, ever her favorite. With a smiling Miss Mittie hanging on to her right arm and radiant Alice clutching her left, Conie receives her guests in the impressive, dark-paneled dining room.

More plump now in her widowhood, Miss Mittie looks like a sausage in pink satin. Alice, exquisite as ever, follows the current popular fashion and actually wears her wedding gown to the party. Small white flowers adorn her hair like so many tiny stars.

At 11 p.m., the exclusive Lauder Quintet, tucked discreetly behind a decorative Christmas screen, begins to play soft music. With one arm tucked behind him, Jack extends his other arm to me in a "Shall we dance?" gesture. I take his hand—it's dry, warm, and pleasant, thank goodness—and we float on a cloud into the ballroom. There we dance for more than an hour.

Jack is a surprisingly good dancer. Not inspired, perhaps, but more than adequate—at least he doesn't "hop" like Theo.

Speaking of Theo, I see that he keeps himself busy all night handing out cigars, shaking hands, laughing infectiously, and serving beautifully as the host of the house.

I dance with Jack, song after song after song. "Away, away, my heart's on fire!" We dance to pieces from the new *Pirates of Penzance* musical theater production and so many more. Sometimes, we trade dances with others, but mostly it's just Jack. I have to say, it feels so *good* to be in the arms of a young man who seems, quite obviously, to be interested in *me*.

At midnight, Jack escorts me to the Morning Room for the champagne supper, catered by Pinard, no less. (Shockingly expensive, but apparently no cost is too much if it helps make Conie's debut a success.)

My mind drifts with the music…

If I'd had a debut party, I wonder what it would have been like.

The thought crosses my mind but briefly. Already, this thought is dim with the dust of time and no regrets on my part. The only thing in my life I *do regret* is what transpired between dear Theo and me in the Tranquillity summerhouse—words that can never be taken back.

WEDNESDAY

5 JANUARY 1881

Last night was my date with Edgar Mulder to the theater … well, at least the show, *Babes in the Wood*, was marvelous. It was very sad, but still enchanting. But what shall I say about Edgar, the quiet young man with the impish smile—a smile that hides such dreadful teeth, poor boy?

Well, he has little to say for himself. *Or* to me.

At first, I try to keep the conversation going, but finally our talk (before, during, and after the play, as well as at intermission) dwindles to just a few words ... and then finally to nothing. When he accompanies me home in a hansom cab afterward, we share a handshake and weak thank-yous at my door—then nothing more.

It's a shame, really. His smile is quite fetching, but he's *far* too shy to speak in complete sentences. He probably doesn't want to show his unfortunate teeth. Alas, dear Edgar ... thank you for squiring me about to a wonderful play. But it's goodbye to poor Edgar. For good.

Thursday

6 January 1881

These days, every Monday through Friday, Theodore Roosevelt II heads over to Fifth Avenue and walks for nearly an hour, all the way to Number 8 Great Jones Street, headquarters of the Columbia College Law School. Here, Professor T.W. Dwight "keeps school" for future attorneys to "read law" in a cavernous old house in the heart of the city.

Even Theo won't go so far as to say he "likes" law school. Actually, I am told that it bores him stiff. What he likes to do—and I've gleaned this much from the Roosevelt girls and occasional comments from T himself—is to research and *write*.

As I've said, he's taking on a huge project, the writing of a scholarly tome titled *The Naval War of 1812*. Whenever he can, Theo steals time away from law school to head over to the Astor Library, where he writes, researches, and then writes some more.

But what he *really* likes, oddly enough … is politics. T is currently hobnobbing with men he calls "rough and tough politicos" at the local Republican Party headquarters. He says he's starting to feel a strong—nay, irresistible—call to get involved with positive social reform on a grand scale—even nationwide. (As he should. There's *nothing* Theo can't do once he puts his mind to it.)

So he stops in at Republican Party headquarters most every day—or, as Theo puts it: "I go there often enough to have the men get accustomed to me so we can start speaking the same language."

I've walked past the big old house on Great Jones Street myself. Twice. I didn't see Theo, but I heard some muffled lecturing as I sauntered past.

Wednesday

12 January 1881

I have — or I should say *had* — high hopes for my evening with Elrod Blake. For one thing, I am wearing a new dress—and heaven knows I don't often get many of those! Plus, I know him enough to know he's a *very* enthusiastic talker, which is definitely to his advantage.

On the night of the musicale, Elrod is *full* of conversation: constant soft-voiced conversation, almost to the point of annoyance; conversation before, during, and after the performances, as well as during intermission. That I will tolerate for the sake of the wonderful music. But that isn't the worst of it, no.

The worst thing is ... he was sweating *so* profusely—and smelling so *abominably*—it was all I can do to "dab" my nose occasionally with a handkerchief ... and then try to keep it there for most of the night.

As he takes me home in a hansom cab, Elrod *does* ask me to go out with him again, but I beg off, saying our family is "probably going to Philadelphia next week for an extended spell to visit relatives," a polite fiction that probably fools no one.

I feel bad—but I *have* to do it. I can't endure another night in proximity to such a stench.

Friday

21 January 1881

Lo, the poor obelisk! It's already relegated to second-page news in the papers. How quickly people forget.

By the time the obelisk was finally dragged to Central Park, it was already this month, the dead of winter, and so far, it's been a nasty one!

The obelisk is positioned on an obscure site: a knoll some yards behind the Museum of Natural History. The site is decided "as per the Vanderbilt family's wishes." (Yes, money talks and loudly too.)

Officials report in the papers today that "the prime advantage of the knoll is its isolation, as it is quite elevated, and the foundation could be firmly anchored in bedrock, lest Manhattan suffer some violent convulsion of nature."

A few days ago, I walked over to see the obelisk in its new location. It was *so* cold and seemed so lonely there behind the museum. Perhaps the long-traveled obelisk now dreams of baking-hot, cloudless Egyptian skies.

The official ceremony for erecting the obelisk will be held one month from today, 22 February. February—ever the bad month.

Yes, I'm more than a little superstitious, and I'll probably *not* attend.

MONDAY

24 JANUARY 1881

Ah, such a shame! I have such high hopes for my date with Percy Mayes. I am *so* looking forward to today at the charity afternoon tea dance on behalf of the "Little Italians" welfare society.

It starts off in a wonderful aspect because—happy surprise!—Percy proves to be a smooth and skillful dancer. I love that in a man! A "strong lead" makes me feel like I can attempt any step, dashing swirl, or dip—and I typically succeed in beautifully following where they intend me to go, so long as they are still holding onto me for dear life—and won't let go.

Perhaps I Will

But it wasn't long after the dancing started when he started to ... what? feel regret?—or remorse?—that he'd ever asked me to this event. (Was *I* starting to sweat abominably?) Because he started looking *constantly* (and eagerly, I might add) over my shoulder to see if someone more interesting than myself (make that another girl) might be heading our way.

Finally, Percy tells me (with poorly concealed boredom), as I return to his company after a visit to the lavatory, "Huh, I thought you must have fell in."

Suddenly, I can't *wait* to get away from Percy, and the feeling seems to be mutual. Like the other fellows before him, Percy hails a hansom cab and helps me step up into its tiny, two-person coach. But that is all—he doesn't ride home with me. He speaks only a curt "Goodbye and thank you, Edith," then closes the door behind me, and waves the driver away. So much for Percy Mayes.

Edie In Love

TUESDAY

25 JANUARY 1881

I read in the *Times* today that two geniuses and two companies are forming a four-way alliance here in Manhattan—Thomas Edison, Alexander Graham Bell, the Oriental Bell Telephone Company of New York, and the Anglo-Indian Telephone Company Ltd. Together, they form an entity they call the Oriental Telephone Company. This new company is licensed to sell telephones in Greece, South Africa, Turkey, India, Japan, China, and other Asian countries.

(What on *earth?! Why?* You may well be asking. We'll have to check back in a few decades and see if this very strange alliance is bringing in new profits and business.)

I think it's a natural progression, however. On the one hand, you've got Alexander Graham Bell with his telephone and Thomas Edison with his megaphone and phonograph on the other … it's only natural that they'd eventually gravitate together to make even *more* money.

I *dearly* wish our family could have a telephone someday ... perhaps, with luck, we will, especially when more people might have them and there might be somebody we wanted to call!

Sunday

30 January 1881

Finally! The last day of a strange but mostly interesting month ... especially for me with four—count them, *four!*—different dates with four wildly different young men. But the *best* of the lot—by the proverbial country mile—was (and presently still is) Jack Traynor Stratton, who takes me out skating today on the marvelous "artificial ice" at Madison Square Garden.

This afternoon skating date with Jack is such a *delight!* I am thrilled to try out the (first of its kind in the world!) "artificial ice." The frozen expanse of this mysterious stuff is very dark and gray, but otherwise it looks and feels the same as regular ice made by Mother Nature.

Dozens of skating couples and singletons flash by us on all sides ... some beautifully gliding and swaying to waltz tunes produced by a tuba, trumpet, and two violins while others staggered about on wobbly legs, clutching the wooden railing along the sides of the enclosure.

While I'm not what one might call a "confident" skater, I can still manage to stay upright and graceful (most of the time) with or without a partner. Because of this, Jack easily teaches me the moves and steps to successfully "skate in tandem."

Once I catch on, it feels like floating! So long as he is hanging onto me, I feel I could do most anything, glide and fly. It was *such* a glorious feeling of freedom.

My afternoon with Jack still enthralls me with its golden glow as he "squires" me home (yes, again in a hansom cab, but this time Jack accompanies me to my door). "May I take you to the new show opening February first, *The Mulligan Guard's Nominee*? For the evening show I mean, not the matinee."

Perhaps I Will

"I'd love to, Jack!" I truly *do* mean the enthusiasm and excitement that rings in my voice.

After "evening shows" will come the kisses that never happen after matinees.

Friday

4 February 1881

Grand Dame Mrs. William Astor is now "quite taken" (make that "dazzled") with the lovely Alice and her irrepressible "Teddy." (And he *has* to answer when Mrs. Astor calls him that, despite how fiercely he hates that nickname!)

A and T are her new "society pets," and after all, her word is society law, so all of Manhattan society now loves them, too.

Mrs. Astor invites Alice and her husband to dinners and soirees at the forbidding Astor brownstone on 34th Street. As her ultimate stamp of approval, she invites T and A to her

January Ball—the traditional climax of the New York social season—and, in case you were wondering, *no*, Mrs. Astor did not invite me. (Mrs. Astor doesn't even *know* me.) Sometimes, I see Theo and Alice cutting wildly through the Riverside and Central Parks in their two-horse open sleigh, Alice looking so Russian yet fetching in her silver fox furs. They look "above the fray" somehow—rich, happy, and secure in their own world of two.

And, speaking of going places with people we'd rather *not* travel with … I find myself more and *more* in the company of Alice. It's such a strange, uncomfortable synchronicity!

I run into Alice while out I'm out shopping for gloves and stockings. I often see her at the theater, usually while I'm attending matinees with Papa. I bump into Alice on my way to lectures, church suppers, informal gatherings at friends' houses, and even, sometimes, during the course of doing good deeds.

My strange synchronicity with Alice continues when Conie invites three of us—Alice,

Perhaps I Will

Fanny Smith Dana, and myself—to accompany her on a girls' visit (Conie called it by that new slang term "girls' getaway!") to Morristown, New Jersey. There (Conie goes on to explain), we four will be able to see the stunning new, Italianate villas, do a little shopping and dining … you know—just "visit!"(Hmm … two nights in a hotel, me and Fanny in one bedroom, Alice and Conie in another. With many misgivings, I still said yes.)

I have to admit that our recent girls' getaway *is* mostly fun and exhilarating, too—lots of laughing, eating way too many desserts, and enjoying the icy blue sky and glittering "dry" snow heaped around the villas—absolutely stunning, even if Fanny Smith Dana does grab my hands and squeeze them too often, saying "Isn't Alice just the *dearest* girl, so lovable in every way!" (As you might suspect, this brings out my Mona Lisa smile for hours at a time.) Everything is fine—or so I think.

But then … as I'm walking next to Fanny, a short distance down the sidewalk behind

Conie and Alice as we window-shop along the commercial district of Morristown, I hear Alice ask Conie in a soft, aggrieved voice (evidently not soft enough): "Why are all of your girlfriends so lovely and friendly to me, but I can't seem to get along with that stuck-up Edith Carow?"

I suddenly feel full of electrical pinpricks. Will Conie reveal my secret yearning for Theo?

Bless Conie's heart, she defuses the situation with calmness and grace.

"Oh, don't take it personally," Conie answers, airily. "Edie means nothing by it, that's just her way … and would you *look* at that *hat*, isn't it simply divine?"

And so the matter is dropped, for a while.

SATURDAY

5 FEBRUARY 1881

So now I've finally had my second kiss from somebody else who isn't Theo.

It happens in the hansom cab on our way back to my house after *The Mulligan Guard's*

Nominee, which was just finishing up a three-month run on Broadway. (I'd give the show a happy B+; although it wasn't very original, it was still good-hearted fun and enjoyable—rather like Jack himself.)

And the kiss?

Ah, the kiss.

Well, it is—different—mostly wet and (dare I say it) kind of frozen yet slimy. But Jack *is* smiling when he does it—I can still see that plainly in the small, dark cab—and so I respond as kindly as possible to his kiss. (His kiss didn't "speak to me" as Theo's kisses always do—or, I should put in the past tense, *did*.)

Yet, I'll be ready for another kiss soon. And then another and another. When the time comes, that is, but I think it's going to be soon! He has already asked me to go out with him to Tony Pastor's Music Hall on Monday night.

Jack begs my forgiveness for being such an "impetuous lover," but his father and uncles are counting on him to accompany them on an "extended sales tour" of upper New York State,

New Hampshire, and Vermont. He won't be back in Manhattan for weeks—no telling how long…

Well, here's to the next kiss! I'll gather them up and treasure them all, as many as I can!

MONDAY

7 FEBRUARY 1881

It's opening night—tonight!—for *The Pie-Rats of Penn-Yann* (a comic re-telling of Gilbert and Sullivan's *Pirates of Penzance*)! *Any* night at Tony Pastor's Music Hall is going to be exciting—you can feel the excitement seeping into your bones from the very *walls* of the place!

Well, the place and the excitement *were* the best part of the show. I find the show itself to be, um, not so much—the silliness was far too exaggerated—but still it is beautifully presented.

And then, again, another kiss happens during our time in the hansom cab—this kiss more assured and confident than the last. It was still just as slimy, still "with no question asked that begged to be answered," but still, I'm happy to take it … and add it to my growing collection of kisses.

He asks me to attend *Billee Taylor* with him next Saturday night.

Before he has to go north with the men of his family, we're packing it all in … as much as we can … (well, up to a point—you know what I mean!)

Monday

14 February 1881

It's Valentine's Day—and "It" is in the society columns today: Corinne Roosevelt and Douglas Robinson are now officially engaged.

If you ask me—and nobody has—Valentine's Day is a poor choice of an engagement date for Conie and Doug, especially because it's around the time when dear Greatheart died and also because of the uneasy relationship between the bride and groom-to-be.

Still, I feel I should note the occasion, so I write Conie a brief letter wherein I mention, "I know I shall like Mr. Robinson, if he will let me, and I rejoice with you in your own happiness, my own dear girl."

What a steaming pile of tripe.

I'm ashamed of myself even writing the words. I know how pressured she feels.

But I'm standing by like a weakling and doing nothing to stop Conie's wedding juggernaut. Indeed, I even encourage her.

Then again, knowing Conie's family situation—plus the fact that she and I are both only "passably pretty" and hardly today's standard of a raving, tearing beauty—I cynically must agree with the majority of Roosevelts who believe Doug is Conie's only chance for marriage, children, and creating a wealthy, suitable household.

It's not exactly the happily ever after that Conie was hoping for. Nor for me, either. *But,* as they say, that's tough … and that's life. We must each navigate our own way through existence by paddling our own canoe.

Saturday

19 February 1881

Three more kisses tonight! And the show is quite something, too! Opening night at the Standard Theatre—*Billee Taylor or The Reward of Virtue*—portrays yet another "nautical comedy opera" like we've been seeing so much of lately. (It's a good thing Jack is paying for all of these expensive tickets—I cannot afford to do so on my own!)

The show came over from great success in London last year, now opening here at the Standard in Manhattan, where it's bound to have great success this year. The London theater critics call this play-with-music a "satiric, cynical, somewhat risqué story" based on a poem of the same title by Richard Brinsley Sheridan, the same who wrote *School For Scandal*, popular a hundred years ago. News is, they're starting to put together a "version for children and families" of this musical production to be ready by this coming spring!

And how did my number of kisses change from one-a-night in a hansom cab to two-at-a-time elsewhere?

Well, I believe … that is, I'm going to fully own up to…

The fact is, it is actually *me*, acting in a shameless manner, who causes this to happen.

After the play, Jack keeps his right arm firmly around my waist as he guides me through the crowds as we move toward the theater exit (after tumultuous applause and encores died down, of course).

I think of the speedy, rattling hansom cabs, bumping over cobblestoned streets—not very good for kissing, truth be told. Right then and there, I decide there is no place like a crowd of faceless strangers to create a small place for us to "be alone in" for a little while.

As crowds press in against us on all sides, I purposely move toward a tight corner of the broad but undulating hallway. Jack follows my lead, his arm still around my waist. As I back myself into the corner while the crowds surge, ebb, and flow before us, I pull him in close to me. *Very* close.

I feel the buttons of his overcoat pressing all up and down my front. I look up at him, ordering myself: *Do it while you still have the nerve.*

So yes, I start kissing him first. All anyone else could see of us (even if they were looking) would be the back of his overcoat.

I feel his initial shock, surprise, and then pleasure as he gladly joins me in the kiss, which eventually became two. Yes, his kisses are still slimy—and mostly motionless—but things feel far more "assured" this time. Two kisses amid the teeming crowd of exiting theater guests. And still, there is also one more kiss in the hansom cab, just so we wouldn't forget how.

SATURDAY
26 FEBRUARY 1881

Jack leaves for the northern forests in two days. He won't be back for at least three months—maybe more.

Just when I'm getting so *used* to him and so comfortable around him. The fact of our temporary parting makes us both a bit somber at the *Mulligan Guard's Silver Wedding* earlier tonight (yes, we saw the *last* of the earlier *Mulligan Guard* show back in early February, when I got my first kiss from Jack, and now they're back with a *new* production—albeit with a slightly tired story—with an opening tonight at the Theatre Comique).

Tonight, there is no chance of a repeat of "kissing in the corner of a crowded room" like before, not only because of the theater's layout but because I am ashamed of myself for being so "forward" last time, and we are both serious about facing the long time when we must be apart. (Yes, there can, and hopefully will, be letters, but Jack admits he isn't much of a letter writer—plus, they'll be traveling so much, always on the go, there will be few places from which they can *receive* letters in return.)

Things are moving so fast for me, these days, that it's making me nervous. *Everything's* moving fast! The DeLesseps Company started digging on the new Panama Canal two days ago. Yesterday, Kansas just prohibited all alcoholic beverages, ever, anytime, anywhere.

I'd like to hole up in a nunnery for a while, stop time from its relentless "running" … and just *think* for a while. I want to think about what I want to do, where I want to go, and who I want to *be*.

Even so, as Jack takes me home in the hansom cab—despite its bumpy ride over cobblestoned streets—we still manage two longish kisses that, despite the ever-present "moisture" and immobility, are still nonetheless cherished, tender, and meaningful. I will miss those kisses…

TUESDAY
2 MARCH 1881

I sigh deeply a lot these days. I know it's mostly my own fault.

To my credit, I grudgingly remove the sheets from my "art pieces" today and make myself work on them for at least an hour. I'm back to writing essays and poems again—but no love stories.

Given an ounce of encouragement, Jack *will* eventually propose marriage when he returns from the north country. I just know he will.

After all, we have kissed now—seven times at last tally.

But I still don't truly *like* the kisses or *crave* them—yes, I *do* like Jack an awful lot, but his kisses, well, they're nothing like Theo's kisses, which are alive, hungry, warm, and always "ask a question." *You* know what I mean. It makes me shudder a little to think about it—sharing a marriage bed with someone who isn't Theo.

It has nothing to do with Jack not being a decent person. It's just that ... he isn't Theo, and therein lies the alpha and the omega of my dilemma.

Sometimes, I start to hyperventilate and think maybe I *do* have to marry Jack. Maybe I *should*. Just like Conie, it's *my responsibility*.

With Mamma ineffectual and incapable, Em young and addlepated, Papa inert and addicted (loving the theater and his bourbon, but not able to hold down a real *job*), there's no one to hold our family together and "keep the papers moving and the money coming in" but me.

If I married money—even just a moderate/modest amount of money—that would certainly alleviate our current strained circumstances. My husband-to-be wouldn't wish to see his in-laws sink into penury, would he?

Then I think of kindly Jack—with his too-close-together, flat-looking eyes, slimy lips, and the way he always, *always* says, "Penny for your thoughts"—and I just can't quite bring myself to do it.

Not just yet.

Perhaps I will, though…

Perhaps I *will*, given enough time.

Jack *is* a good man, and I *do* like him—but he deserves someone who loves him for *all* of his own stellar qualities, not just for his pleasant temperament and free tickets to Broadway shows.

Just yesterday, Em and I ran into Alice, Bamie, and Theo at a newsstand, of all places. As we chatted together about this and that, T finally divulged: "I'm abashed and ashamed of myself because even though I try faithfully to do what Father has always done, I do it so poorly! I'm learning that we each have to work in our own way to move toward our best. I know I'll eventually follow with Father's good works and do what he'd have me do … I just need to do them in my own way."

THURSDAY

3 MARCH 1881

I learn a secret from Bamie. It's Theo's secret, and he's desperately trying to keep it from everyone—especially Alice—but it shows all over his face: he secretly *hates* law school. It's so mind-numbingly boring and splendidly, irredeemably dull … ugh.

These days, it's only Morton Hall that keeps him going, keeps him alive! The headquarters for the Twenty-First Assembly District of New York's Republican Association, Morton Hall, is also known as the Club for the Silk Stocking District. Silk Stocking, yes. I suppose it *is*, with its tony neighborhoods, including Theo's just a few blocks away.

Apparently, the political riffraff at Morton Hall present themselves as a breath of fresh air to Theo. Oh yes! I have this straight from Conie. Apparently, he can't help slinking off and spending hours there each day with coarse men of the lower classes, whose lives revolve around politics (both the clean and dirty varieties).

Sometimes (if it happens to suit them and their circumstances), it even involves social reform and progressivism. To Theo, I know this sounds like Heaven on Earth. Wild horses couldn't keep him away from something *this* enticing!

Even after an evening at the theater, Theo still often makes time to dash out—stylish and out-of-place in his expensive evening suit—across Fifth Avenue, round the corner of 59th Street, and then up the shabby flight of stairs.

I'm told that Morton Hall is a big, old, drafty chamber located over a store. Or maybe a barroom. (I need to slowly walk past it, one day soon, and see what I can discern from the outside.)

Although I don't see Theo very often, I *do* sometimes run into him in the oddest places ... poetry receptions and musicales, old rare bookshops, and men's haberdasheries (where, when our family feels flush, I sometimes look for a new shirt for Papa). Though he seems a bit guarded with me, he's still perfectly cordial.

In brief words and anecdotes—sometimes punctuated with his irrepressible laughter—he sketches out the scene for me; vividly, my mind's eye sees the rough benches and spittoons where low-class attorneys, along with Irish bar keeps and horsecar conductors who run T's district, get together for frequent political meetings. They don't even need an official meeting, really, because every night it's like a men's clubroom in there—thick with blue-gray cigar smoke and plenty of loud, good-natured arguments, mostly delivered with an Irish accent.

Of course, Theo's family is horrified. The Roosevelt family—and I, when he has a spare minute for me—continue to urge Theo to "maintain prudence" in his political life, to "maintain an innate distrust of the so-called public life," especially after the way professional politicians treated dear Greatheart. To think Theo actually wants to go and *associate* with such men … who are so rough, brutal, and unrefined … and *work alongside* them.

I admit that I look a bit askance at this new side of Theo's career aspirations myself.

But when I venture to ask Theo about it , he just scoffs and then grins so that his teeth gleam like a young colt's in the daylight.

He poo-poos such notions as "milquetoast."

"If this were so, it merely means that the people *I* know in politics happen to belong to the governing class, and besides, don't worry … I intend to *be* one of the governing class. I won't quit until I've made the effort and found out whether I'm too weak to hold my own in the rough and tumble of politics." Theo has a private score to settle, too. It's with the so-called "New York State Republican Machine," still controlled by Boss Roscoe Conkling, who ultimately destroyed Greatheart, body and soul. I'm hoping and praying that this younger Roosevelt, by mastering political techniques and applying his considerable savvy and influence, can use that same "machine" to avenge his father eventually. I know that Theo always carries some of his father's old letters in his coat pocket as a "talisman against evil."

Perhaps I Will

Friday

4 March 1881

Inauguration day! Today, the humbly born James Abram Garfield will officially become America's twentieth President. Chester Arthur is his new vice president. Theo knows "Debonair Chet" very well from his time at Morton Hall.

When none of the "establishment" candidates could get enough votes to secure the nomination, the delegates chose Garfield as an "unpopular compromise" on the thirty-sixth ballot. *Nobody* is too excited about Mr. Garfield becoming president. It's not a great way to start four years of a presidency.

Sunday

13 March 1881

Shocking news from around the world comes to us via telegraph and now on the front page of the *New York Times*: Tsar Alexander II, son of Nicholas I, has been assassinated. No idea yet about the assassin and his motives. As Papa in a surprisingly lucid moment said at breakfast: "There's going to be hell to pay for this ... just you wait ... it could mean another European war." Dear Lord, let us *hope* not! But I think we've not heard the last of it yet.

Monday

18 March 1881

Yesterday at this time, *I* didn't wheedle Conie about "taking her somewhere to cheer her up." This time, *she* invited *me* to join her in cheering *me* up.

With me, Conie make no bones about it. "I want us four girls—Bamie and Em, me and you—to go to the opening of *Barnum & Bailey's Greatest Show on Earth* right here at MSG tomorrow!" (That's what real New Yorkers called Madison Square Garden; MSG.) "You need to get *out* of your house, away from good deeds and just go somewhere so as not to think, but just to *laugh* and enjoy! It's my treat for you and Em as belated Valentine's Day presents."

She's right. It's been quite a while since I've laughed about *anything*. It's definitely a date for the four of us.

The "artificial ice" at MSG is long gone now—at least until next winter—and the great B&B extravaganza has taken over the entire property, making it into their version of a "Roman Hippodrome." It does me *so much* good just to giggle, eat pink cotton candy, and not "think" for a while as we hugely enjoy the animal tricks, men on the flying trapeze, death-defying stunts, slapstick clowns … even the world famous Jumbo, said to be the largest elephant in the world. The famous elephant cost Barnum *$10,000* just to ship it over here from the London Zoo! (P. T. Barnum swears he's confident he *will* get his "elephant investment" back in profits from ticket sales—we shall see!) I thought the poor, massive elephant looked very sad myself; no doubt he was dreaming of blue African skies and humid air.

Monday

28 March 1881

More and more, Theo is moving to the forefront of Republican Party politics. His name makes the newspapers with thrilling regularity.

While I still go out regularly and do good deeds and create sub-par oil paintings, uninspired charcoal sketches, and reams of essays, Theo tells the women in his family he still "can't *believe* his good fortune to win the fairest, purest, and sweetest of women!"

But, protestations to the contrary, I can tell that Theo is *also* getting "restless."

How do I know? Because of how he reacts when listening to Elliott's letters from India, extolling the heart-pounding excitement of his tiger-hunting there.

I happened to stop by West 57th last Saturday morning (dropping off my book of Swinburne poems for Conie to read and borrowing her Washington Irving's *Sketchbook* for myself) when my visit suddenly coincides with that of the postman.

Miss Mittie exclaims shrilly when, amongst the letter pile, she discovers an envelope with stamps from India. "Oooh, it's Dearest Ellie! Come to the sun parlor, everybody, and I'll read it aloud!" Conie and Bamie move briskly toward the sound of their mother's voice. Even Theo and Alice appear from somewhere in the depths of the house. Unobtrusive, I follow them all to the sun room.

As Miss Mittie reads the letter aloud, detailing glories of the hunt and steamy, alluring India, Theo starts pacing, up and down, down and up, round and round the room.

I know he's desperately longing to join in the hunt. Theo yearns, ever and always, to heed the call of the wild.

"You're acting like a caged lynx!" Alice complains "Please don't pace!"

Quickly, I utter my thanks for the loan of the book, take my leave, and exit the house with speed, just as Theo starts soothing Alice with kisses, reassuring her that he's having just a "momentary lapse and longing" for wide open spaces.

I know he misses ... well, *so* many things. Collecting live and botanical specimens, for one. For years, he and I did that together in perfect symmetry and happiness; I never minded the slime or mosquito bites or walking through mud—none of that bothered me one bit.

Back then, Theo was free to do and be, to come and go as he wished. I also sense that Theo misses our years of convoluted, lengthy literary and intellectual discussions.

And I wonder...

Friday

1 April 1881

I knew we hadn't heard the last of it. An article on today's front page of the *Times* describes how Russian cavalry soldiers are running roughshod over Jews—both urban and rural—

killing, burning, pillaging, and much worse. "It's the Jews who were behind the assassination of Czar Nicholas II," government representatives pronounce to the foreign press. In Russia, they're calling the cavalry raids "pogroms," which is said to mean "a little bit of thunder" in Russian. Already, many Russian Jews are trying to flee the Russian empire, and many hope to join relatives soon in New York City.

Tuesday

12 April 1881

I've received two letters back from Jack so far—I sent him several letters in care of a certain lumber mill office in Buffalo, New York. I'm not sure if Jack received them or not. His two letters so far don't mention receipts of any letters from me.

I've gotten very good at keeping a stiff upper lip these days *and* smiling my ever-present Mona Lisa smile. Because wherever I go, whatever I do, I *still* keep running into Alice Lee Roosevelt. Shopping in the same stores, often dining at the same dinner parties, attending the same theater performances—last night Papa and I encountered Alice and Theo exiting the theater after opening night of *Little Nell and the Marchioness* at Abbey's Park Theater. It was a very good show, actually.

SUNDAY

24 APRIL 1881

Something totally out of the *blue* happened to me today—I'm still tingling with (and unnerved by) the shock of it. Theo invited me to spend the afternoon with him in Riverside Park—thigh to thigh with him in his tiny dog cart.

Alone.

It's rather shocking for a married man who is about to embark on a second, extended honeymoon trip with his bride! (His *real* honeymoon, that is … the first honeymoon, the Tranquillity honeymoon, was just for practice. Literally. The second honeymoon will be in Europe for five long, lovely months.)

Alice had *just* left to visit her parents for a spring vacation at Chestnut Hill when who should send me a note but Theo, asking if I'd go riding with him tomorrow afternoon (actually today), together in our favorite park, "just to talk" and get caught up on old times.

I tell Mamma I'll be out at the Lenox Library, perusing several of their new acquisitions, and I'll be back well before nightfall.

When Theo comes to call for me, I head him off halfway down the block. Readily I take his outstretched hand and spring up into the tiny-yet-tall conveyance.

It's as if no time has passed between us at all.

We drive through Riverside Park, chattering and joking non-stop. We take turns dissecting poems, the good and bad, some old and some new, including our mutual favorite, "King Olaf," by Longfellow.

We even sing songs, including the current popular tune "My Bonnie Lies Over the Ocean." Theo can't sing worth a lick, but for once, my high, tinny voice rings true. "Oh, bring back my Bonnie to me!" I carry his voice along with mine in a pleasing duo.

I can't help bringing up a truly large "elephant in the room"—that being the fact that Theo and Alice will leave on 12 May for the five-month European honeymoon.

I'm *so* eager to go to Europe myself someday (somehow) that I can't help gushing: "Oh, be sure and see Big Ben for me ... and the Louvre!"

"Come see it for yourself sometime!" He nods to make a point. "You'd adore Europe—so much history and art."

As if *I* could ever afford to go to Europe in our present strained circumstances. Yes, I know my family goes to the theater a lot, but we almost *always* sit in the cheapest seats. So I just roll my eyes at him, and he knows enough not to pursue the subject further.

Toward dusk, after a couple of hours of non-stop talking and horse-walking, we let Lightfoot rest at our favorite Riverside Park viewpoint.

Remaining together in the dog cart, speaking little, but feeling and thinking much, we watch the sailboats move about, seemingly aimless, on the blue-green waters of the Hudson River. The sky is a pinkish pearl, with hues as glorious as the inside of an abalone shell.

It is *so* good to see Theo "up close" again—I mean, *really* close up. He's not wearing his glasses today, for some reason, and I take care to memorize his features in their present form: the two waves of rusty-brown hair against his forehead and a small mustache over his beautiful upper lip (the lower lip is equally beautiful, exact mirror images of each other). I memorize his funny "mutton chop" side whiskers, bushy and reddish—I hope he'll outgrow *that* phase soon. I love to gaze at his long, straight, serious brows and into the depths of his blue eyes beneath.

Dear God, I've *missed* him so much! Much more than even I realized.

I've missed the closeness of just us two … our private "knowingness" … our own select world where we need no one else.

I feel a sudden internal pang and feel myself mentally "curling-in upon myself," like a bird with a broken wing.

All my thoughts—good, bad, or indifferent—about Jack Trayner Stratton or any other young man vanish instantly, like dust on the wind.

Oh, dear heart, I don't think I can stand it anymore.

Nobody knows me like Theo. No one else understands me nor appreciates my mind and intellect like Theo.

No one else in the world is *like* him. No one else in the world can *replace* him. No other man in the world can make me *laugh*—like Theo.

With glittering clarity, I now—silently—admit, affirm, and avow that I am now, and always will be, a one-man woman. Theo is, and always will be, the only man in the world for me.

I simply don't *want* anyone else. Is that *also* going to be the "waste of a good woman" (me)? Um, probably. But I'm not going to go there just now. I'm just *not.*

And if he cannot be mine, well then … so be it. I'll continue bush-whacking my way through this world on my own. (I won't be the first and certainly not the last woman to do so.)

Still, I feel like the weight of decision has finally fallen from my shoulders. I don't have to look for the right man anymore. I'll simply go it alone.

(No more free theater tickets...)

I summon a broad but closed-lipped smile. I manage, albeit tremulously.

"So, Edie…"

T looks at me with a mixture of yearning, dismay, concern, and buried emotion. He's leading up to questions I won't want to answer. "Dear girl … are you not encouraging your suitor, Mr. Stratton, to continue his pursuit of your affections—oh yes, I heard about him. And if not, what are you going to *do* with yourself?"

Hmph. That's not exactly the question I expected. I *thought* he was going to ask if anyone has asked me to marry them.

I was aiming to look "free and easy," independent and confident, not an object of pity and worry.

At least I can tell him what I'm doing with my time. That's an easy answer.

"I'm following in dear Greatheart's footsteps—in whatever small ways I can, of course—volunteering at the Newsboys' Lodging House and Children's Aid Society, Miss Sattery's School for Little Italians, and the Five Points Mission. There are always worthy places that can use more help. I figure that *somebody* in society really needs to help out—so why not me?"

It's getting on toward evening now. I can hardly see his face in the dim light. He just replies, "Hmm … lofty and noble ideals, indeed. I just hope you won't wear yourself out in the process."

Sounds to me like he *wants* me to be married to someone else, just to let him off the guilt hook.

He clucks to his horse Lightfoot, gives him a gentle slap of the reins, and says, "Let's sing our way home, shall we?" Without waiting to hear my answer, he starts in on another popular song—this time, the newly published old Scottish lament, "Bonnie Banks of Loch Lomond." His off-key singing voice begins with a froggy undertone: "By yon bonnie banks and by yon bonnie braes, where the sun shines bright on Loch Lomond…"

I finally chime in with him for the chorus: "Oh, ye'll take the high road, and I'll take the low road, and I'll be in Scotland afore ye! But me and my true love will never meet again, on the bonnie, bonnie banks of Loch Lomond…"

What *are* we singing? Suddenly, the words hit way too close to home. "Me and my true love *will never* meet again" … at Loch Lomond or anywhere else.

We ride the rest of the way back to my front door in a fraught silence.

THURSDAY

28 APRIL 1881

Notorious old west gun slinger Billy the Kid escapes from two jailers at the Lincoln County Jail in Mesilla, New Mexico Territory, killing two men before stealing a horse and high-tailing it out of town. Yes, this news tidbit was on the lower left corner of the front page of the *New York Times* today. New Yorkers love to follow the careers of gun slingers, card sharps, and notorious horse thieves—much better than boring local gossip and twice as colorful.

THURSDAY

12 MAY 1881

This morning, T and Alice will embark on the steamship *Celtic* for their five-month honeymoon in Europe. Or, as Theo tells anyone who will listen, "I'm off for a summer abroad with my dearest, little wife!"

I elect *not* to "wave them off," as so many

other friends and relatives are doing. I'm strong enough to do many things in my life, but not strong enough—nor fool enough—to do *that*.

Law school closed its doors for the summer last Friday.

The political hacks of Morton Hall will have to do without Theo until sometime in October. (*October* ... eons away.)

Yesterday, Miss Mittie ordered the blinds to be drawn for the summer at West 57th in preparation for Miss Mittie, Bamie, and Conie—along with their contingent of servants—to begin their summer residency at Tranquillity on Oyster Bay.

Conie told me yesterday: "Theo seems to be going a thousand miles a minute, even dictating a will (now that he has a wife to leave his fortune to!) and to pack a thousand pounds of luggage to bring across the sea."

It's going to be a long ... and, I daresay, arduous ... summer for me—I can just tell.

No letters from Jack in a very long while.

S̲a̲t̲u̲r̲d̲a̲y̲

21 May 1881

Today in Dansville, New York, the wonderful Clara Barton founded the American Red Cross to help and protect sick and wounded during war and natural disasters. How I wish I can volunteer at her organization! Alas, for now, all efforts are coordinated from the upper New York state office. This remarkable woman risked her life to bring supplies and support to soldiers in the field during the Civil War, nursing, cooking, and comforting the wounded, earning the nickname the "Angel of the Battlefield." I'll be waiting and watching to see if they'll soon open a chapter of the American Red Cross in New York City anytime soon.

Sunday

22 May 1881

H*a!* Conie wrote me that, on their sea journey to Europe, Alice was "horribly seasick and utterly helpless," and Theo exhausted himself taking care of her, night and day.

What a pity he didn't marry a girl with *gumption.* Someone who could take care of herself—and him, too.

THURSDAY

2 JUNE 1881

After Conie and I attend the wedding of Lucille Goodman (former member of our P. O. R. E. writing group), Conie decides to write "her Doug" all about it. *But…*

As Conie confides to me today, "I started out with my usual salutation to Doug—you know, like I always do: 'Dear Old Fellow'—and, at the end of the letter, I started to sign off with 'Yours, Conie, your own little girl.' But then I crossed out that last part and wrote below: 'I don't like the idea of being anybody's except my own.'"

Conie's face clouds up just then. I look back at her inquiringly, and she explains: "You *know* that my walking down the aisle means renouncing my own autonomy."

There's no rejoinder to that. She's right.

Conie faces a gathering cloud of challenges after her marriage. First, there's the groom himself, a good man but too often ill-tempered, and one with *no* interest in the hurly-burly of politics (while Theo, Conie, and Bamie all seem to crave and thrive on it … Miss Mittie, Elliott, and I, not so much).

Then there's Mother Robinson, her mother-in-law-to-be, a formidable battle-axe who tyrannizes her servants and even physically assaults them.

Another challenge will be the changed status of her own financial inheritance, which, after she marries, will come totally under her husband's control.

Soon, Conie will live her entire existence within somebody else's shadow: Doug's.

Perhaps I Will

WEDNESDAY

29 JUNE 1881

I haven't received a letter from Jack in an everlastingly long time. I've stopped writing to him because he evidently got tired of writing to me—unless, of course, his letters went astray...?

Ten months from today, 29 April 1882, Conie will marry Douglas Robinson and start her grown-up life.

A sobering thought—for us all.

But, until that portentous day, Conie and I are becoming closer than we've been in *years*. We're like sisters.

We're *better* than sisters. (*Much* better—I think of hapless, heedless, hopeless Emily, whose non-stop talking is worse than ever. She continues to grow—up and up—until she's now four inches taller than I am.)

I know Conie is afraid of life "changing too quickly" for her. And here *I* am, fretting that my life might not change at *all*—or, if it does, it might be a change for the worse and not for the better.

Most every day—when I'm not doing charitable tasks—Conie comes over to my house or I head over to hers. We read, walk, talk, window-shop, and sometimes even ride the Roosevelt saddle horses in Central Park.

Conie confides to me her deepest sorrow: "I know I am destined to live and die *without* romantic love. And now, it's looking like that might be the case for *you*, too."

SATURDAY

2 JULY 1881

Madness!!!
Today's afternoon newspaper headline reads: "A Frightful Calamity for America!"

A deranged man shot our new president today with a pistol he'd hidden in his suit-coat.

In office only these last four months, President James Garfield only started getting used to *being* our president. Now he is fighting for his life after the attempted assassination.

He was shot at close range in the Baltimore and Potomac Railroad Station (of all places) at 9:30 a.m. today by an enraged job-seeker named Charles Guiteau, who vowed revenge on the president for "not securing a patronage appointment" for him, "even after he gave me his solemn promise he would do so. He callously lied, and I was ruined!" Our president still lives … for now. We'll see how strong is his mettle, how tough his constitution. Can he make it through this current nightmare and fight his way back to a decent state of health and strength?

Friday

15 July 1881

Famous western outlaw Billy the Kid, age twenty-two, was shot and killed yesterday by Sheriff Pat Garrett, age twenty-one, outside of Fort Sumner in New Mexico Territory. (In about three weeks, I will be age twenty-one myself!) The Kid "met his demise" around 12:30 a.m. when he went to his friend Pete Maxwell's home in Fort Sumner in search of a slice of beef for a late-night snack. Well, at least no one can say that *I* am "living fast and dying young." I'll probably live to be an old woman with a life where nothing much happens ... except I'll just get more querulous and vague. I'll have cats, no doubt. Lots and lots of cats.

Wednesday

20 July 1881

More news of the Wild West—and very sad news it is.

The great Sioux Chief Sitting Bull, most noble among the warriors, surrendered to U.S. troops with the last of his band of fugitive people (estimated at less than two hundred souls).

No more would they attempt to run to freedom in Canada. They were all too tired, hungry, desperate, and exhausted to try anymore.

Theo and Alice are somewhere in Italy, now, I believe. He'd have no way of hearing of this poignant happening in the last days of the Old Wild West.

Saturday

6 August 1881

Today I'm officially an old maid.

Today is my twenty-first birthday, and anyone would agree that I'm now *way* past "the first bloom of youth." There wasn't much celebrating of this fact within my family. Aside from a couple of weeks' rest at Grandfather Tyler's summer place, we've kept mostly quiet this season.

Mamma is even more morose and distant than usual.

Emily keeps chattering, more and faster, to fill any silence. Papa, well, he just gets quieter and drinks all the more—it breaks my heart to see his habitual hopeless, resigned look. Going to the theater with me doesn't even cheer him up the way it once did.

Even dear old Mame sighs deeply and stays closer to the kitchen than before. At least we've managed to hire part-time help to assist her with the family cooking and cleaning.

Conie sends me a birthday letter from Tranquillity. The P.S. at the bottom of her letter says it all: "I wonder if we will always be so placed as to see much of each other as time passes. But the future is very secretive, and on the whole, I am *glad* it is secretive. I *don't want* to know what's coming."

I don't either.

MONDAY

19 SEPTEMBER 1881

The presidential assassination finally succeeded. President James Garfield died today, eleven weeks after being shot by the enraged spoilsman.

Vice President Chet Arthur succeeded him as president.

I feel so off-kilter—unsettled, nervous, and uncertain of the future. Can you imagine these crazy times in which we live? When some stranger with a gun can actually *kill* our own, current, sitting president? What *happened* to our safe, reliable, and honorable country?

Where has it gone?

Will I ever feel anything like normal again? Let alone happy again?

Saturday

1 October 1881

A body—well at least a body like *mine*—can only fret, fear, and worry so long. Then, in spite of myself, the feeling starts to lift and dissipate.

Life goes on. And I, too, start flowing again carried by life's inexorable current...

…and look what life's current brought to my shores now. Alice and Theo are back again. He's *home!*—just a couple of days ago.

I don't know if Jack Traynor Stratton is home again or not. Maybe he is. Perhaps he's wandering out there in the world, I know not where. I sure wish I'd hear *something* from him, though. I don't want to contact his family business yet—not just yet, but maybe soon.

While in Europe, Theo continued to peg away, day and night, writing *The Naval War of 1812*. Now that he's back, he's even resuming the dreaded law school. It's dispiriting for him, and for me too, just by thinking about it.

Thursday

6 October 1881

I now have an extra-special reason to read the newspapers because Mr. Theodore Roosevelt II is sometimes mentioned therein.

The "Silk Stocking" Twenty-First Republican

Assembly District (who I privately call The Gang at Morton Hall) is now going through its annual machinations to "send the strongest, toughest assemblyman possible" to the state capital at Albany in January 1882. T is smack dab in the thick of everything, of course, working on what his faction of The Party needs him to do, especially if it's along progressive lines, about which his faction is lukewarm.

He *thrives* on the "rough and tumble" of politics, despite his family's objections to such a dirty business.

Right now, the Republican Party is split into two factions. I couldn't care less, except for the fact that Theo is in the middle of it, and I need to keep abreast of who is who and what is what.

Monday

24 October 1881

Just so you know ... little (if any) of this made it into the papers. Most I just heard from

Theo himself as I join a recent Roosevelt family gathering after a theater matinee.

Here's what Theo says really happened:

At a pre-convention meeting in Morton Hall, Theo stands up to make a formal protest against the nomination of one Mr. Trimble for assemblyman. According to Theo, Trimble is a "machine" man, a sniveling individual who follows the same old party line—same as it's ever been.

Morton Hall bosses Jake Hess and Joe Murray listen to Theo with freshly "opened" minds.

Joe Murray already has enough delegates to nominate whoever he wants, even if Hess doesn't like what he's saying, so this is what he tells his cronies (like it or lump it): "The bad old days of Republicanism are *over*. This boy, Theodore Roosevelt II, is the son of 'Thee' Roosevelt the First, one of Manhattan's most revered philanthropists and do-gooders who ever lived! He's got everything we need; he's an Ivy League man who can bring in the swells and the university crowd. As a knickerbocker with a long, illustrious history, he can help drum up funding from along Fifth Avenue. Sure, he's like a child about politics, but he's learning fast. Plus, he simply *glows* with righteousness! He'll be independent of any political machine and immune to all bribes. He is honest, elegant, humorous, and a born fighter. He even enjoys getting up onto a chair and shouting at people! I say it needs to be TR—or no one."

And so, just like that, the eldest son of "Thee" Roosevelt is selected as the Republican candidate for assemblyman. They're going to nominate him on 28 October 1881.

Thee's eldest son is the *one* Republican who can keep the party's seat in the state legislature out of the clutches of the opposition.

Thursday

27 October 1881

It's T's 24th birthday today, but the news on everyone's lips this morning is the so-called

"Gunfight at the OK Corral" ... a shocking, thirty-second blood-bath that occurred yesterday in Tombstone, Arizona Territory. The Earp Brothers—Wyatt, Virgil, and Morgan, along with their friend Doc Holladay—went up against a gang of ruffians called The Cowboys, readily identified by their red sashes. When the gun smoke cleared, over thirty bullets had been fired in just thirty seconds, and three of The Cowboys lay dead.

This news certainly stole (some of) the thunder from Theo's upcoming nomination tomorrow!

Friday

28 October 1881

Well, it's finally official: the day after his twenty-fourth birthday, Theo is the official, nominated Republican candidate for the New York State Assembly in the Twenty-first District.

Perhaps I Will

I am thrilled to the *skies* for Theo. He will take the dirty politics and make it a vehicle for reform and justice. I just *know* it.

I also know it's the start of something big for Theo. It's something *huge*, portentous, noble, inevitable, and unavoidable.

While Conie and Bamie are thrilled with Theo's nomination, Miss Mittie is still of two minds about it. The various uncles and male cousins in the Roosevelt clan look askance at one another. Privately they tell Miss Mittie that "Theo is making a massive mistake!"

Tuesday

8 November 1881

Today is voting day—and now, all the nail-biting is over for me ... over for us all. Theo *wins*.

Yes! I can't help being wild with joy. I'm wild on *his* behalf, and Alice has nothing to do with *anything*.

He went in early this morning to vote (we heard later), and then he rushes back home to work on his book, which is due at Putnam and Sons, Publishers by Christmas.

As of tonight, dear Theo has been officially elected to the New York State Assembly, where he aims to become a leader of the reform faction of the Republican Party.

So now it begins. Again, my heart crinkles with foolish love for him all over again.

Saturday

3 December 1881

Today is the day Theo must hand off his weighty book manuscript to Putnam and Sons, Publishers, even on a Saturday. (They gave him a couple of extensions earlier, but no more!) I hope *The Naval War of 1812* makes its deadline.

Perhaps I Will

Tuesday

6 December 1881

Days fly in a whirlwind.

Now that Theo and Alice must soon move away to Albany—known to New York society as Outer Mongolia, so *fearsomely* far away—the golden couple are fêted at balls, dinners, receptions—you name it, they're at the center of it. Because Alice leaves tomorrow on an extended visit to her parents in Chestnut Hill, I'm hosting a party for Theo tomorrow night as well. (Just for *him alone* and his unique accomplishments—*not* for her.) As before, I'm making it a political victory celebration for T with all of the same friends who came to my earlier party, except even more this time.

Yes, the cost of this gala is putting a *massive* dent in our household budget for December, but it's nothing I can't shuffle and manage (reimburse) somehow. To Mamma's hemming and fretting, I keep soothing her with the following, hypnotic refrain, "Hush now, Mamma, I have it *allll* under control." I do—mostly. If I find myself running out of available funds afterward, I'll just take a few pieces of silverware ... a superfluous gravy ladle here, a couple of serving spoons there ... to Kircher & Sons, Ltd.; they're very discreet, pay a decent rate for silver products, and never ask me questions. Papa never asks me about anything to do with money; he simply goes with the flow and keeps quietly sipping his bourbon.

Because they must stay in Albany for so long, Theo and Alice decide to remain at West 57th for the time being, instead of purchasing a home. Although Theo must stay mostly in Albany, Alice can move between Albany and Manhattan as she chooses. With Miss Mittie, Bamie, and Conie for company, Alice will have plenty of women to watch over her and chatter with. When the State Legislative 1882 session concludes in late spring, then the happy couple can start looking for a different home of their own.

More good news! In just a few short days after its release, *The Naval War of 1812* garnered *superb* reviews, with great praise for its "scholarship, sweep and originality, along with extreme detail."

From Theo, I'd expect no less.

2:42 a.m. on Friday
9 December 1881

A glorious success!!!

My party for Theo was a rousing celebration here at home tonight at "East Thirty-Sixth" (Carow's), enjoyed by all thanks to the ministrations of discreet servants (rented for the night), a caterer with two assistants, and even a three-piece band (two violins, along with a French *artiste* performing popular dance tunes on the old upright piano in our parlor).

Theo's companion for the night is his mother, Miss Mittie, and Conie and Doug are there too. Oh my goodness, in person Doug is a mountain of a man—so tall, dark, and shambling, with sloping shoulders and huge hands (with a few wiry dark hairs growing above the tendons.) He seems to be a man of few words—cordial yet unoriginal. He keeps looking to Conie (for approval, perhaps? Or reassurance?), and she looks back at him with what I perceive to be stretched-thin patience with a veneer of politeness.

Elliott is still in India hunting tigers, but Bamie is her usual confident, magnetic self tonight.

Fanny Smith Dana is here, too—still hanging on Theo's every *word* and giving him nothing but praise and approbation no matter what he does or says; I hope she remembers that she's a married woman to another man. (Her husband is currently based at the Brooklyn Navy Yard, just a bit too far for him to show up tonight.)

Still caught in the thrall of his weakness for the latest styles, Theo wears a bright, satin waistcoat and leads the cotillion dances in his usual "springy" style. I manage to snag him for a couple of dances. Just like old times, we laugh so much, exulting over the positive direction his life is taking.

Perhaps I Will

Only three more weeks, though, and Theo and Alice must move 135 miles north to the state capital at Albany for the opening of the 1882 State Legislature. They won't be home for months.

At one point tonight, Miss Mittie confides to me that she dreads parting with Theo and Alice, "who has endeared herself to me and is *so* companionable, always ready to do what I ask of her. I *do* love her, and I think she loves me."

How "nice" for them both, I'm thinking in a rather nasty mental tone, if I do say so myself.

I should be thoroughly ashamed of myself, but just now, I can't seem to work up the effort to wash my thoughts in righteousness.

When my dinner party finally concludes around 2 a.m., Theo shakes my right hand, over and over in both of his—it feels so good to feel his warm, slender fingers encircling mine!—in endless thanks. He proffers no hug or embrace—that wouldn't be proper coming from a married man—but still, his eyes speak volumes to me. I know that *he* knows I wish him only the *best*, like a prayer: now and always, forever and ever, world without end. Amen.

New Year's Day

1 January 1882

Theo invites a gang of us—girls and fellows both, most of whom I don't know—to hop a train to Montreal, Canada, and meet up with Alice, who is already there.

Who could refuse a prepaid, three-day New Year's excursion in an exotic foreign city (well yes, I *know* it's just Canada, but still…) and gratis lodging in an elegant hotel?

Certainly not me. Alice and Theo are going to be gone all winter long—I must absorb as much of his company as I possibly can while the offer still stands.

When have I *ever* said no to a chance to bask in Theo's grinning, hilarious (albeit platonic) company?

Certainly not lately.

Especially with no words—yea or nay—from Jack Traynor Stratton. I'm definitely sending him a letter in care of his family lumber business.

Monday

2 January 1882

The whirlwind weekend is winding down. Today, we split in three different directions. Alice remains in Montreal for another two weeks with a large, hilarious "party of friends." Theo takes the train to Albany for the opening of the 1882 legislature. The few of us remaining—myself and one other wallflower, Annie Murray—now head for home. (Where else?)

Alice will train down to meet Theo in Albany in two weeks, where, together, they'll look for "suitable marital lodging."

In the meanwhile, Theo told me he's making a bee-line for the Delavan House, an old, rambling, shambling hotel with a fantastic restaurant right across from the train station. (It's very popular with bachelor assemblymen with hearty appetites.) They say that New York's new state capitol building is one of the architectural wonders of the nineteenth century. Some critics even term it a wonder of the world!

Dazzling in white granite, the new capitol building looks (in pictures, anyway) like something out of imperial India. Just imagine: it cost $11 million—yes, that's *million*—dollars to build it, so far. And it's still not finished yet!

Saturday-Sunday

7-8 January 1882

Theo returned to Manhattan for a quick weekend home ... his first as an official politician!

Alice still "plays with her friends" in Montreal and then will head to Boston for a while to see her folks. Elliott remains abroad. Miss Mittie has neither the aptitude nor appetite for discussing the finer points of politics. So Theo happily talks for hours to Aunt Annie Gracie and me this weekend in her cozy brownstone at 26 West 36th Street. (Although I don't crave necessarily to hear about politics the way Bamie and Conie do, I certainly crave Theo's company—and that's enough to keep me listening, rapt, by his side.)

He keeps telling Aunt Annie and me, over and over, "You *do* know, of course, that I'm not *really* going into politics. I just want to … learn things that'll help me later on when I begin a *real* profession."

Although he won't admit it to us, I know Theo feels a bit "knocked back" by comments made about him and his fancy garb that immediately started rattling around the Assembly Hall.

Theo admits to us, though, as he tries to make light of it, that some of the men are starting to call him—and to his *face*, mind you!—epithets like Jane-Dandy, Punkin-Lily, Weakling, Young Squirt. Or the worst of all: a Damned Fool.

I'd like to kick their teeth in—talking to such a smart, earnest reformer in such a manner. They don't know what a treasure they've got in their midst. They're the *fools.*

TUESDAY

10 JANUARY 1882

Oscar Wilde ... yes, *the* Oscar Wilde, internationally famous Irish playwright, poet, and lecturer—just twenty-eight years old, seven years older than me!—reached U.S. shores a few days ago to start a coast-to-coast lecture tour at New York City.

On Christmas Eve, he left from Liverpool heading to America on the S.S. *Arizona* bound for New York. The reasons for his much-heralded visit to the United States are (first) to promote Gilbert & Sullivan's latest operetta *Patience* (prepaid to him by G&S with a great sum of "marketing money") and (second) to give a series of lectures (paid for by individual ticket sales) on subjects "of his own choosing."

Perhaps I Will

I *knew* this was one celebrity—*a man, an actual individual,* not just a celebrity—that I wanted to see, but I decided to attend his presentation as a singleton. Conie could care less, and Papa doesn't like anything on stage unless it's a sentimental drama or musical comedy. So off to Chickering Hall I go, several days early—corner of Fifth Avenue and 18th Street—to buy my advance ticket for last night's performance.

I have to tell you … I find myself *deeply mesmerized by Oscar Wilde,* and I'm adoring every minute of his presentation. Just looking at him and listening to the cadence of his voice is deeply pleasing. Oscar Wilde himself has an Irish-lilted voice; he's so very handsome, unusually tall, very lean of frame, with thick, waving brown hair bobbed at jaw length.

Well, you could have heard a pin drop, so entranced are we all by his presence as well as by his presentation. Every seat at Chickering Hall is taken early, and scores of folks are left with "standing room only."

Here's part of what the *Times* wrote about him in this morning's edition: "A Large

Audience Listens to the Young Aesthete: Talking in a sepulchral voice to wondering men and women—finally, an opportunity to laugh that was readily seized upon by the audience regarding Mr. Wilde's views on poetry and criticism." The news article goes on about the "many representatives of families conspicuous in the fashionable world … several Protestant clergymen and one Catholic priest … young men dressed themselves as if for an opera … and ladies attired in rich costumes were numerous."

He delivered his lecture on the "English Renaissance." (I didn't know there even *was* one. I thought it was all in Italy.)

I can tell you this—I am entirely, thoroughly, and genuinely grateful that I was able to get a seat for Oscar Wilde's first performance in America! What an honor and a supreme pleasure.

I love his wit, which includes these favorites:
Be yourself; everyone else is already taken.
I can resist everything, except temptation.
I have nothing to declare, except my genius.

Wednesday

15 February 1882

The hazing is getting worse all the time.

I'm getting all this third-hand, of course—from Roosevelt relatives, acquaintances, and even from the papers—that now Theo's "hazing" is turning *ugly*.

Some assemblymen seek to humiliate T, especially a big brute called Big John MacManus (ex-prizefighter and Democratic Party Tammany Lieutenant), who recently pronounced to his politician co-workers: "Let's toss him up in a blanket because his sideburns are just too ridiculous for words!"

Fortunately, T received advance warning of this in the midst of installing Alice into a rented house in Albany. When he hears this, does he shake in his boots? Not the Theo *I* know! (Not so it shows, anyway.) Instead, T marches straight up to MacManus himself, who towers over him like Goliath, and tells him the following— verbatim. (As well you might imagine, I did *not* read this in the papers. I overhead Theo's cousin

Emlyn tell it to a college comrade in *sotto voce*): "I hear you're going to toss me in a blanket. By God! If you try anything like that, I'll kick you and then I'll bite you—in fact, I'll bite you in the balls!"

Yes, he said *balls*.

And he said more than that: "I'll do anything I can think of to you—and I *can do* it too, you know that I can!—so you'd best leave me alone."

You know how relentless Theo can be when he means business. The bully MacManus backed off, muttering to himself. Here's another ugly incident, one that proves Theodore Roosevelt II is *not* a young man to be trifled with. With a fashionable cane tucked under one arm, wearing doeskin gloves and a ridiculously short pea jacket (known in the British vernacular as a "bum freezer") T strolls along Washington Avenue in the capital city with a couple of political comrades. They stop at a saloon for sandwiches and are immediately confronted by a tall, imposing fellow named J. J. Costello. (Wouldn't you just know it—*another* evil Tammany kingpin, hated and feared by all who know him, and there he is, trying to get Theo's "goat.")

Costello immediately taunts Theo before the crowd that's starting to gather: "Oooooh, won't Mama's boy catch cold?" Of course, he stares at Theo's … well, at his posterior. (I don't know any other proper term to call it.) Anyway, it was not covered by a proper length of coat. It was just … well … out there.

So Costello kept saying it and *saying it* in a cooing, teasing voice, while he stared and chuckled.

But you do not mock Theodore Roosevelt, the Harvard second-place lightweight boxing champion.

Theo slugs him across the jaw, despite the fact that Costello is a head taller than him.

A surprised Costello tries to struggle upright, and Theo punches again. The tall Tammany henchman falls over like a wounded turtle. He wallows about on his back, then manages to right himself, and lunges at Theo.

Theo slugs him a third time.

Finally, none too gently, Theo stoops over and jerks Costello upright. In the presence of many wide-eyed onlookers, Theo admonishes the bully, "Now you go on over there and wash yourself off. When you are in the presence of gentlemen, you must *conduct* yourself like a gentleman. Good day." With that, T strides away, his two friends following behind … leaving an admiring, astonished crowd in his wake.

Tuesday

7 March 1882

When a tide turns and starts to flow in, you generally notice it pretty fast. Theo's displays of physical courage definitely turned his tide, just like that. Increasingly, he's becoming the man of the hour—sharp, bright, enviable, and capable—nobody's fool.

The papers have a heyday when Theo starts denouncing State Supreme Court Justice Theodore Westbrook as a co-conspirator in a railroad investment scandal, one which destroyed many legitimate—and innocent—investors.

Most of the assemblymen—like so many bleating sheep, spineless creatures!—try to evade Theo's demand for an investigation. I'm not surprised when T outmaneuvers them with brain-power and skillful verbiage, securing the right to finally investigate.

Alas, the evildoer *still* manages to evade justice. However, even though the crooked judge side-steps everything—even though sufficient incriminating evidence doesn't materialize—Theo's "stock still shoots up quickly," according to his peers. They now treat Theo as someone to be reckoned with, which he is.

Wednesday

29 March 1882

While I am thrilled to the skies with Theo's burgeoning courage and fearless ambition, not everyone in the Roosevelt family is pleased about it. Far from it.

Edie In Love

The family unrest now comes to a head.

Bamie and Conie relate to me in shocking detail what happens when "Uncle Jimmy" takes Theo to a private lunch to straighten him out.

"You've done well in Albany so far, and it is a good thing to have dabbled in social reform. But, dear boy, it's now time for you to start identifying with the right kind of people. In short, it's time for you to *leave* politics."

Then, Conie adds to me her own editorial "asides."

"Uncle Jimmy thought *surely* Teedie would back down and defer to his wishes. But never! All Brother said was, 'So do I always, then, *have* to yield to corrupt people?' Uncle Jimmy admitted that there will *always* be a secret inner circle of corporate executives, politicians, lawyers, and judges who control *everything*—and who always obtain the real rewards. And then, without being rude to Uncle, but still standing up for his rights, Theo said he still had much reform work to do before he was through with politics."

Perhaps I Will

Monday

3 April 1882

Most newspaper reporters think Theo is absolutely *wonderful*. One reporter wrote that Theo's "most refreshing habit was actually calling men and things by their right names," while another declared, "This young reformer is going to have a splendid career." Still another called him "The Cyclone Assemblyman," with admiration and envy.

Although I secretly agree with Uncle Jimmy that politics is a dirty, nasty business, I'm the first to admit that Theo was *born* for the politician's role. He's fearsomely smart, a speed reader with a photographic memory, as well as a *voracious* reader of all sorts of books.

Even when he is thwarted from meting out justice to the crooked judge, Theo is not afraid—nor discouraged. He speaks to the Assembly in a slow, clear, trembling voice, "You cannot by your votes clear this judge, even as you cannot cleanse the leper. Beware lest you taint yourself with his leprosy!"

You *tell* them, Theo! You tell them what they so desperately need to hear!

THURSDAY

12 APRIL 1882

Charles Darwin, the infamous "monkey man" and author of *On the Origin of Species,* died in England yesterday at age seventy-three … and...

...on that same day I finally received a letter from Jack Traynor Stratton.

In it, he apologizes for the "very long delay" between letters—to say the least!—but he writes surprising news:

> *My father wanted me to run a branch office of Stratton & Sons Wholesale Lumber Inc. based out of the community of Lake Placid. I went into this project with good intentions but soon lost my heart to the Adirondack Region. I could no longer*

see clear-cut logging as commensurate with the highest and best good of that region. Many persons around here want this area turned into a permanent park for all posterity.

I am now working with a group that is helping to set aside the Adirondack region as a park for New York State, as is Yosemite in California.

As you may presume, my father and uncles are highly displeased with my choice of a profession because it does not include the felling of trees but instead saving them. However, there is no money to be made by saving the forests as they are. Thus, I have to work on the side to bring food to my table. My side job is now as railroad timetable clerk, and as you may guess, there are no theater tickets in my life just now, nor likely to be any in my future. But helpful legislation and protection is getting closer all the time to a permanent protection for Adirondack Park where these forests should be set aside and preserved.

I cannot participate in any clear-cut forestry, and that is the chief task that my father and uncles still wish me to do, so we have parted ways, to my great sorrow, regret, and pain.

I keenly miss our times together, especially our times at the theater.

Someday, if I ever return to New York City, I will definitely renew acquaintance with you. In the meanwhile, I wish you the very best in your future life.

Your sincere friend,

Jack Traynor Stratton

I have no words...

SATURDAY

15 APRIL 1882

Life is moving like a millrace these days. Too many worries, wonders, facts, and fantasies whirl in my brain like my own private cyclone … including the exceedingly shocking and private fact that Alice has been having "nervous spells" with ever-increasing frequency.

She wants a baby *so* badly, but something is wrong inside so a baby can't "take hold" and grow.

According to Conie's divulged confidences, Alice and Theo discuss possibilities of surgery for hours on end. The doctors promise it will help, and she's agreeing to do it. Though she dreads and fears both scalpel and anesthesia, both of them yearn for a child of their own. And *soon…*

…and then there's our beloved upcoming bride, Miss Corinne Roosevelt, who is marrying Doug in less than two *weeks!* She's scared *stiff,* poor thing.

There's no one she can talk to concerning the mysteries of marriage. Miss Mittie changes the subject immediately if Conie dares ventures a word. Besides, I heard Miss Mittie tell her own sister Annie, "Well, nobody told *me* in advance, so I certainly don't need to tell *her.*"

In my mind's eye, I think back to the mating act of the two dogs—my own dog Ruby and an eager, interested stranger ... so long ago, now! When I think of what those dogs did, it doesn't seem so revolting to me, at *all.* It's certainly nothing to be afraid of, provided you're with someone you love. It might be a bit strange, yes, and rather odd, but still somehow ... thrilling.

But what if you *don't* love your partner? Conie doesn't love Doug a *bit.* And all that *I* want is—

Never mind what I want.

It's not so much what I want but what I'm allowed to have—and what I *have* right now is the role of bridesmaid, one of eight, at my best friend's wedding. I go in for final fittings of my bridesmaid's gown next Tuesday.

But mostly what's bothering me these days are the *songs!* They're driving me crazy.

The new popular songs are just *everywhere* nowadays. They are embedded deep in my own brain, and I can't get them out. Relentlessly, the catchy refrains play over and over, those of the "Whiffenpoof Song:"

"We're poor little lambs who have lost our way…

Baa, baa, baa.

We're little black sheep who have gone astray.

Baa, baa, baa…"

The song goes on to intone, "Gentleman songsters off on a spree," which thankfully doesn't resonate with me because I've never been on a "spree," whatever that might entail.

But the rest of the words trouble me. They pierce me to the core:

"Doomed from here to eternity…

Lord have mercy on such as we,

Baa, baa, baa."

I can't help it—I must implore in prayer: *Ah, Lord, please have mercy on such as we. On such as me.*

Each in our own way, we're all doomed—Doug and Conie, adrift amid marital fears and a lack of love; Theo and Alice, seeking a baby they can't seem to kindle; even me, with my good works, family responsibilities, and all those children I'll never have…

Lord have mercy on such as we.

There are heaps of other popular songs out there these days, mostly happy songs like "The Skaters Waltz" and the irresistible "Sweet Violets." Undeniably, though, the most popular song out there now is "Goodbye My Lover, Goodbye."

Don't even get me started on *that* one…

Enough journal writing. I must save my strength for managing to plow through the Robinson-Roosevelt wedding without disgracing myself.

Perhaps I Will

10:40 P.M.

29 April 1882

Conie married Doug Robinson today at the Fifth Avenue Presbyterian Church, just four months before her twenty-first birthday—a very late wedding for a "rich girl."

I have to tell you … Conie spends most of her wedding ceremony weeping and snuffling.

It embarrasses even me the way Conie keeps carrying on. Miss Mittie is simply *furious*.

It could be worse—a *lot* worse.

Doug and Conie have *some* commonalities. Both are superb riders, loving their saddle horses even more than they do many people. At heart, grumpy old Doug is a decent—and very rich—man. Plus, he's a surprisingly good dancer, despite his undeniable "tummy." And he's a true and loyal friend to Theo and Elliott.

This day, one that I thought could never materialize, has now come and will soon be gone. I still see it all so clearly in my mind's eye:

As one of eight bridesmaids—mostly school friends, including Fanny Smith Dana, along with Alice and Bamie, plus some cousins—I see myself, standing motionless beneath a bower of palms and smilax in the nave of the church.

The minister's voice holds me in its thrall—just the way a wedding celebrant's should. His voice is austere, yet kind, detached somehow, and seeming to examine some secret sorrow of his own.

"I now pronounce you man and wife. What God hath joined together, let not man put asunder. In the name of the Father, the Son, and the Holy Ghost."

Then he pauses (not dramatically, I think, but almost pityingly). At last, he intones slowly and with a gentle sigh, "World without end. Amen."

I start to quiver and cannot stop myself, even by locking my knees. My trembling may soon be evident if I don't nip it in the bud, but no one is looking at *me*, thank goodness.

It's so … final. Isn't it? World without end, amen.

Perhaps I Will

I glance briefly over at the groomsmen, standing with uncharacteristic soberness in a row at the other end of the altar.

I look at Theo, second from the left. He doesn't catch me watching him; he's keeping his eyes on the minister.

World without end for Theo and Alice, too.

After the wedding reception at the Roosevelt mansion, when it's time for Conie and Doug to leave on their honeymoon, we eight bridesmaids lead the half-hearted bride into the sun parlor, now set up as a changing room with all doors firmly shut.

The other bridesmaids hover, giggle, and coo in excitement, enough to set my teeth on edge. It's all I can do to keep the other girls from detecting my quivering.

I can't get those words, *World without end, amen,* out of my mind.

I paste on my Mona Lisa smile and remain mostly quiet among the other girls' chatter. Along with the others, I'm going to help Conie out of her wedding gown and into her going-away outfit—a stylish, blue-gray wool gown and matching coat, trimmed with silver fox fur collar, cuffs, and muff.

Two ladies' maids lift her starched, muslin gown over her head and uplifted arms. They carry it away to be safely boxed and protected from moths until Conie produces a daughter who might wear this gown at her own wedding someday.

Conie stands, frozen-faced and trembling, in her steel-cage crinolinette, made in the latest fashion: a starched-fabric, steel-ribbed hoop-skirt frame, like an upside down vase. (Whoever dreamed this old Civil War fashion would be revived and updated in modern 1882?)

I reach for both of Conie's hands to steady her, as the other girls fuss, fidget, and fasten her into the fashionable woolen gown, matching coat, and silver fox hat, collar, and cuffs.

Conie's hands are ice-cold and clammy in mine.

"Promise me…" she pleads through chattering teeth. "Promise you'll write me at *least* once a week, especially once we move to Orange?"

(That's Orange, New Jersey, where Doug's family has an impressive mansion set aside just for them in which to make their marriage nest.)

I promise her I'll write. It's a promise I'll keep.

I can't look Conie in the eyes when her groom, Doug Robinson, comes to lead her away to an enclosed barouche parked outside.

It isn't a very cheerful letter that I write to her today when I begin my first missive to her—me as an official spinster and she as a married woman.

I write: "During your wedding, I kept realizing that you were leaving your old life behind, and even if we live to be ninety years old, we can never be two girls together again."

I can't bring myself to speculate, let alone attempt to write about or even *think* about Conie's wedding night. Whether she will cry or plead for more time alone. If he's going to scold, scowl, or struck something with his fist. (Not her, though—I could never conceive of Mr. Robinson doing something dastardly like that.)

But I'll never know, will I?

World without end. Amen.

THE EXACT DATE DOESN'T MATTER ANYMORE.

MAY 1882

All my school friends are pairing off and getting married. I realize that I am ... so very ... very ... lonely.

I find myself relying on my own family more for company, on Em and Mamma, and even on dear old Mame.

Miss Mittie's sister, Aunt Annie Gracie, is even more an angel than usual to me now. She *knows* I'm adrift in my life, trying hard but going nowhere, especially with Jack Traynor Stratton in upstate New York working to make Adirondack Park an official reality, so she takes great care to invite me to join her for theater matinees, the symphony, or art receptions—anything and everything.

I am pitifully grateful to be asked and say *yes* to anything she proposes.

Friday

2 June 1882

Today, I learn by accident that Theo and Alice are heading for Tranquillity to spend the summer there … along with Miss Mittie, Bamie, and Elliott. Even Doug and Conie are coming for a spell.

I wonder if Theo ever takes Alice rowing in his rowboat—the one with the name *Edith* painted on the stern.

Perhaps he has painted over the old name. Maybe *Alice* emblazons the boat now. I'm guessing her name is in blue letters against a yellow background.

Tuesday

1 August 1882

I want to remove myself as far as possible from the white-pillared reminder that is Tranquillity. There are too many memories in that beautiful home by the sea—painful, tender, and unbearable. It's just too full of Alice, Theo's beautiful bride.

So, this month, when Grandfather Tyler asks Em and me to join him in Canada at St. Hilaire Mountain Resort near Montreal, we won't be asked twice. The prospect of blessed *escape* and an all-expenses-paid trip to someplace new is irresistible to Em and me both.

I only wish St. Hilaire were located in San Francisco. Or Hawaii. Maybe even in Hong Kong. Halfway around the world would be better instead of just a short ways north into Canada.

Grandfather invites Em along as a courtesy to Mamma. Because my mother is literally the "least fortunate" of Grandfather's five children (financially speaking and in most other ways too), he's giving Mamma a little breathing space, away from her annoying but still unfortunate younger daughter, as well as her prim spinster older daughter—both of us social failures.

I know Grandfather can barely endure Emily, with her nail-biting and cuticle-picking, too-frequent horse laugh, ubiquitous nervous gasps, and endless chatter about supposed suitors (all imaginary, as far as I know).

Mamma is going to stay quietly at home with Mame, along with our portly new cook (hired just last month) and our new (sadly frog-faced) housemaid Patterson, to keep an eye on Papa. The plan is for Em and me to stay in Canada with Grandfather for the entire month of August, including my birthday. Even longer, if we can manage it. After all, what do we have to come home for? To come home *to?* Certainly not school—or husbands of our own.

I suspect Mamma looks forward to time away from us too, even as we do from her.

I know for a fact that Grandfather Tyler loves me dearly. He's always telling me that I'm his "favorite grandchild," even within earshot of Em, which makes both of us feel uncomfortable—and sad.

But I can't help loving my maternal grandfather back. He's such an honorable man and a dear, even if he *was* the one who generated the ridiculous—and horribly fateful—idea that "Theo and his family suffer from scrofula."

Those words separated the dear boy and me forever. Grandfather harps back to this fact frequently, forgetting he's already mentioned it so many times: "Dear Edith, how *glad* I am that you didn't marry that—that diseased young Roosevelt. If you only realized how truly, deeply proud I am of you—just the way you *are, without* a husband! *So* proud of your literary talents, your skills with painting and sketching, excellence with your studies, and now your good works on behalf of those less fortunate…"

Grandfather sighs deeply, whether in admiration or relief, I don't know. He leans in confidingly to me with an air of one imparting a great secret.

"I'm here to reassure you, now and always, that you needn't think you *have* to marry *anyone*, dear girl. Instead, just devote yourself to whatever appeals to your noble heart! Because…" Then,

Perhaps I Will

Grandfather Tyler's hooded gray eyes mesmerize mine with the depth of his love—and by the financial power he holds over us, benevolent as it may be. "By means of the inheritance I'm going to leave to your mother, and ultimately to you girls, you needn't worry about crass financial matters *ever again*."

I feel like squirming under his gaze; with difficulty, I refrain.

Yes, I certainly *do* know about this coming money. I've nursed this shamefully reassuring knowledge to my bosom for some time. I rely on this nugget of knowledge to ultimately save my family—financially—one day. Grandfather Tyler amassed a large personal fortune, which will be portioned out, upon his death, amongst his five children.

It's a blessed relief to know he's going to endow Mamma with part of his fortune when he dies. All we have to do is be patient and worthy and endure our strained finances a while longer.

Tuesday

5 September 1882

I hear a sound like the soft roaring of the sea.

Now it's getting louder, and I can't imagine what it could be.

Suddenly, I remember! It's the ten thousand workers ... laborers, tradesmen, working women like cooks and housekeepers, too ... all coming together, marching down the street, holding banners and placards, marching in support of workers *everywhere*—the very first Labor Day Parade in the history of our nation. The soft roaring sound is made up of the collective sounds of cheers, whistles, clapping, and cries of support.

If I remember correctly, I think they're supposed to be marching down Fifth Avenue—close enough for us to reach in minutes. I snatch up my hat and rush out, grabbing Em along the way. I want to watch the workers, and I want to remember this day.

This is something we hope to tell our grandchildren about—providing we have any, that is...

Wednesday

13 September 1882

Em and I have been home now for a couple of weeks, and Grandfather writes me the following note, which brings tears to my eyes. I place this letter carefully in the top drawer of my dressing table to keep always—so I can refer to it, again and again.

His letter is brief: "Old age, my dearest Edith, as I know by experience, requires much patience and consideration on the part of those who 'administer to its wants'—that is *you*, my dear!—and who are sometimes sorely tried by the caprices of old age. The only recompense that remains for you is the 'conscious discharge of your duty,' to be repaid back to you, perhaps in kind, in due time, when your own old age will overtake you."

I keep this letter as a talisman—and a sign from above—that I am here in this life to do my duty, above all else, to those who need me. This letter reminds me of my highest reason and purpose for living.

Thy will be done—divine will, not mine.

Thy will for me is not so much that "I shall live," but rather that "I shall serve."

Friday

15 September 1882

I can't do it. I *won't* do it.

I was going to write about something that's troubling my heart—what else is new?—but it's too depressing to stumble about to find the right words, especially when nothing ever changes.

Perhaps I'll feel better in October.

Until then…

FRIDAY

27 OCTOBER 1882

Today is my beloved's twenty-fifth birthday—and Theo's and Alice's wedding anniversary. They must be having some kind of a party, but maybe it's only for family. (Of which I am no longer an honorary member.)

Maybe in November, I'll feel more in the mood to write about things … other than just Roosevelt things.

I keep thinking that something is going to change … that something *must* change … but nothing ever does. Gray day follows gray day on and on into an endless future...

THURSDAY

9 NOVEMBER 1882

I'm feeling better this month. The gray fog of depression is lessening. I'm not sure why or how...

Last month, Theo and Alice joined the ranks of Manhattan homeowners—they bought a small but exclusive brownstone row house at 55 West 45th Street. (I walked by the place recently but took care not to "tarry" while rubbernecking. Of course, I've not yet been inside—and probably never will.)

Fanny Smith Dana is already a frequent visitor to the love nest (wouldn't you *just* know). I'm willing to bet that she, too, still nurses her long-held yearning for Theo, despite her marriage to a respectable older man. But all she'll admit about *that* is to avow that the Roosevelt brownstone "is so full of fun and talk."

Much of the "talk" must buzz around the fact of young Mr. Roosevelt's rising role in politics. Theo has just been re-elected to yet another term in the New York State Assembly.

I hear via the high society telegraph that Alice was "bored" in Albany during the legislative season, so she's only too thrilled to return to the verve and tang of Manhattan. She's even brought two maids with her—and now doesn't know what to *do* with them. Aunt Annie is literally (and most kindly) drawing up a list of maids' duties for the new, fledgling household.

Fanny is annoyingly adamant about it to me: "You should really go over sometime and see just how *happy* Teedie and Alice are, spending evenings together in their cozy sitting room before a bright soft-coal fire, with Teedie's books all around them as they play cards or backgammon."

I ignore Fanny's well-meant but obviously outrageous suggestion.

Thursday

30 November 1882

Our front doorbell jangles ominously. A half-grown boy in a Western Union cap and jacket announces: "Telegram for Carow." (And when has *that* ever been good news?)

It's not: dear Grandfather Tyler is dead.

He collapsed early today at the Fifth Avenue Hotel in the city—of all places. Miraculously, all of his children and grandchildren happened to be here in town; we all hovered around his deathbed with tears and mourned his passing.

He died without ever regaining consciousness.

Already, it's been decided that his body will be taken in a special funeral train south to Anniston, Alabama, the town where he grew up, and over the same railroad tracks he caused to be built so many years ago during his railroad business days.

It's anticipated that the number of mourners will exceed two thousand, maybe more, as befitting a man of consequence, which Grandfather Tyler certainly was.

A cache of money will soon be Mamma's—and *ours*. It's not to squander frivolously, no, but to make our simple lives less full of care, penury, and hounding by bill collectors.

I say a fervent prayer of thanks to Grandfather on behalf of us all.

Perhaps I Will

Friday

1 December 1882

Thomas Alva Edison has gone and done it again (this time with help from his trusted assistant, Edward Johnson)! They've invented something *nobody* ever thought of before—something nobody ever dreamed of or wanted. But now, all of us want one for our Christmas tree: electric, colored Christmas tree lights!

The holiday lights designed and produced by Mr. Johnson consist of a long string of electrical wires, fastened together with unobtrusive ties, with many tiny white electric lights shining from inside of different colored glass "bulbs."

The tree is notable enough to be written about in newspapers this morning, and by tomorrow, everybody is going to want one—just wait and see!

TUESDAY

5 DECEMBER 1882

Not so fast.

We're *not* getting the money after all. At least, not in the way that Mamma's sister and brothers are receiving their portions.

I'll explain.

Of Grandfather Tyler's five children, four each will receive cash payouts of $47,000. But *not* his daughter Gertrude, my mother.

I should have known that Grandfather Tyler was no fool. No way he was going to release a large sum of money—free and clear, no questions asked—to his dithering daughter Gertrude and her cultured but nearly penniless husband Charles Carow.

Through Cruikshank and Sons Financial Advisers (who have long helped the Tyler fortune mushroom most gratifyingly), Mamma herself (with me managing the money)—and *not* Papa—will receive two $2,500 semi-annual interest payments against a principal amount of $47,000. Upon her death, the interest will continue to be paid to granddaughters Edith and Emily.

The principal cannot and *will* not ever be touched, per the existing legal document.

Ever. (At least by no one in *our* lifetimes.)

How simultaneously mortifying, yet gratifying.

Rapidly, I add up long columns of numbers in my head—mental debits and credits of our family's income and out-go—and then divide the total by twelve months.

I breathe easier. Yes. Though the interest money is not large, it still truly *is* a blessing and most timely, too.

After paying off our various, longstanding lines of credit—something I've wanted to do for years and lived in shame that we couldn't do before—we'll be able to live on this bequest adequately when we add it together with Papa's monthly "work subsidy" from the Carow brothers.

The constant worry that usually furrows my brow finally dissipates.

We shall do *fine*.

So long as property taxes, the price of soft coal, water and trash collection, plus groceries don't start rising too fast…

Two days after New Year's
3 January 1883

According to the *New York Times*, yesterday a man named Isaac Hunt stood up at the Republican caucus in Albany and offered the name of Theodore Roosevelt II for Speaker of the Assembly. A flood of cheers, punctuated by whistles and shouts, erupted instantly.

Everyone adores Theo so much, there was no need for a vote. I'm told this process is called "vote by acclamation" in political circles.

The dear boy is rising like a rocket—even the sky is no limit for the likes of him! To think that only a year ago in the Assembly, he was derided as that "damned dude" and a "pantywaist." Now most everyone—overtly or secretly, depending

Perhaps I Will

on one's party affiliation—looks to him to be both savior and leader, the Republican Party's choice for the most prestigious office in New York state, aside from that of governor. Even if the Democrats still carry the day—which they probably will, for a host of reasons—that's still all right. Theo is on his way.

Even though he's the youngest man in the New York Assembly, he's utterly fearless as he forges ahead with reforms to lift the lives of average New Yorkers out of the muck and into the light. He's fighting to establish a much-needed park in Albany and to finally put some teeth into penalties for men who abuse women and children.

There'll be nothing and no one who can stop him now—Lord willing.

Monday
8 January 1883

The New York social season of winter '83 is exploding like a 4th of July fireworks display this year! Already the city's social calendar is filled to overflowing.

It's like we've all been waiting for something to happen—some vague permission to be granted for hedonism and pure pleasure, perhaps ... and now, evidently, something has triggered this license for permissive behavior in all things. So many expensive people are behaving in very expensive ways these days, and folks seem to thrive on it. It's all so daring and dashing—ah, to be young and living in Manhattan during the winter of 1883. Yet, the *New York Times* continues to report that our nation's financial depression of 1882 is continuing on into 1883 ... I guess poverty and business depression can mean different things to different people.

(Or to *feel* young, at least ... I'm not considered among "the young" anymore.)

Perhaps I Will

Already, I've seen the great actress Lily Langtry—up close, too!—when I went with Aunt Annie and a group of her friends backstage to congratulate the British beauty on her masterful performance. Langtry was then making her first American appearance at Wallack's Theater. The actress is every bit as striking as everyone says, but her crystal, gray-blue eyes are unnerving … they are *so* much like Alice's.

Certain dance bands and orchestras are so popular these days they must literally dash between engagements in Philadelphia, Boston, Providence, and New York, ever on the run to catch trains to their next dance venue. Sometimes they play for three different parties in a single day.

Known for playing as hard as he works, Theo returns to the city most every weekend to, as he puts it, "drink the wine of life with a splash of brandy in it." Alice doesn't *have* to come back for weekends because she's already here full time. I hear Alice finds plenty to keep her occupied in the big city.

Whether a subscription or regimental ball, a play or concert, opera or private musicale, theatrical performance or groaning nine-course dinner, Theo immerses himself in each activity with gusto, his beautiful bride on his arm, as he flashes crowds with his irresistible, toothsome grin.

Tonight, even Aunt Annie Gracie entertains guests as she features an "amateur dramatic" in her home. The guest list will include the "usuals," among them Theo and Alice, of course; Fanny Smith Dana and her husband; and yes, ever the proper spinster, Edith Carow, dressed in a re-trimmed green satin gown from three years back.

Even Em is invited to the party. She'll probably end up not going, though, because she's currently suffering a "fit of nerves" and is sipping a supposedly restorative "tisane," thus far with little success.

Wish me luck. Or at *least* wish me someone to squire me around when it's time for the "light supper" after the musical performance.

Perhaps I Will

I keep hoping that Jack can return to the city again … someday … once the state of New York can legally repossess the six hundred thousand acres of Adirondack private property with back taxes still unpaid. With all of those beautiful acres *finally* at the state's disposal, they can—and will—create a magnificent, permanent nature park. Then Jack can come home…

Theo's dream of building an imposing hilltop house on his own acreage grows ever closer to reality. The bride and groom are now "studying plans" for a grand, new residence on Long Island. What is new with me, you may ask? I'm in a right proper rut, but there's no one else to do the house management except me. I still manage the family bookkeeping, purchases, and payments. Thank goodness we no longer have to "rob Peter to pay Paul," as we did for more years than I care to admit.

True, although our home spending is far from lavish, *most* of the financial tension that ravaged our family for years has disappeared, thanks to Grandfather Tyler's bequest.

However, our family budget remains a delicate balancing act as it grows ever more expensive to live in NYC.

The newspapers are starting to call it inflation.

I also keep my poor father company, mostly during twilight time.

Poor Papa—he looks, frankly, terrible these days: so pale and waxy, with persistent pain under his left ribs. Yes, he's still drinking and taking laudanum. We still talk about the theater (although he isn't up to going anymore; he's too weak and tired).

We still read books together, mostly read by lamplight, during which Papa frequently expresses a yearning for "our whippoorwill" to come back. It is highly unusual for a whippoorwill to nest anywhere in New York City, but this one does, nesting—and beautifully, poignantly vocalizing—on our front window ledge in the spring. (Alas, spring is still many months away…)

I've become more accepting and nurturing of Mamma and even Em these days. Their lives are even more depressing than mine. There's a strange, unsettled feeling in our house. I can't quite put my finger on why.

At least I've come to value, more than ever, one special person—Aunt Annie Gracie—for the angel she truly is.

I know she feels sorry for me, carrying as I do my double burdens of being not only a spinster but a wallflower. Bless her heart, Aunt Annie goes out of her way to invite me to art exhibitions, concerts, Bible readings, birthday parties—you name it.

And I accept all of the invitations with unabashed gratitude.

I am unashamedly *grateful* for her kindness.

On a lighter note—and *speaking* of notes, musical or otherwise—the silly new song that's all the rage now, "Polly Wolly Doodle All the Day," circles round and round in my brain, like an eel in a lagoon. How I *wish* I could drive this annoying tune out of my head, but it just won't go.

Edie In Love

Oh my gal Sal, she's a spunky gal
Sing polly wolly doodle all the day…

Fare thee well, Fare thee well
Fare thee well my fairy fey
For I'm goin' to Lousiana
For to see my Susyanna
Sing polly wolly doodle all the day

(Oh yes, I'm spunky, all right … a spunky gal, that's me.)

Enough of this—I won't write again until I have something amazing and worthwhile to write about. (Seeing as that would literally be a miracle, who knows when *that*'s ever going to happen.)

Perhaps I Will

Friday night, snuggled in bed with my journal.

2 February 1883

It's finally happened: my miracle out of the blue.

It's likely to change my entire *life* around from top to bottom.

No. To put it more accurately, it could easily *lift* me from the bottom of the pile up to the very top.

Here's how it happened, moment by moment:

This morning, I hear the doorbell ring (as usual) and the mail-drop cover clattering (as usual) after the postman slips a modest allotment of Carow mail through the slit in our front door.

I'm sitting at the dining room table, making a list of bills due the first of this month. I figure and fiddle over which can be paid now (most of them) and which of them, alas, must wait. (Yes, it's February 2nd and I'm already a day late, but I figure the banks are closed until Monday, anyway, and so...)

I give the mail no more thought.

That is, until Mamma comes to where I sit at the table as I mutter and add numbers together under my breath.

In her right hand is an elegant-looking letter—a square, ivory-colored envelope, heavy stock, most expensive.

Mamma's right hand trembles. Her voice trembles, too, when she quietly asks me: "Why is the richest woman in America sending a letter to *my* daughter?"

"What?" I'm too stunned to even sound properly surprised. I take the letter from her outstretched hand and examine the return address: Mrs. W. K. Vanderbilt, 660 Fifth Avenue, New York City, New York.

The Mrs. Vanderbilt … the matchless Alva Erskine Smith Vanderbilt herself … a would-be queen of New York society, with so much money, nobody knows just *how* much; it piles up faster than anyone can count it properly.

Why on earth is she writing to *me*?

Perhaps I Will

My own fingers quiver when I grasp our old, tarnished letter opener—a trusty tool handy for opening bills—and use it to open this elegant missive.

"My very dear Miss Carow," I start to read aloud in a quavering voice. Mamma listens with pinpoint attention. Even Em appears from nowhere, eating an apple and eager to glean some good gossip.

(Oh, this has *got* to be plenty good gossip, all right—what on *earth?*)

My voice grows stronger and more excited with each word I read.

From an excellent and reliable source, your name has been recommended to me as one who represents the noblest, highest, and best of 1883 young womanhood from among the finest families of our fair city.

You are invited to join a select gathering of young ladies and young gentlemen (along with triplicate understudies, one hundred of you in all) to perform in one of six select quadrilles at my upcoming Ball of the

Century, a fancy-dress ball to take place on Easter Monday.

The six quadrilles will include the Hobby Horse, the Mother Goose, the Opera Bouffe, the Star Quadrille, followed by the Dresden, and concluding with the Go-As-You-Please. You are invited to participate as one of the four principal ladies dancing in the Star.

A guest list of more than twelve hundred is anticipated, including the designated four hundred members of the Patriarch Balls, and will include the most refined and exclusive individuals in the city.

Because several practice sessions will be required of all dancers (including the young ladies, young gentlemen, and all understudies) to perfectly perform their own quadrille by the night of the ball, we require that we hear from you at your earliest convenience, whether you agree to perform in this capacity or whether you regretfully must decline. If we do not hear from you by 15 February, another young lady will be selected to dance in your place in the Star Quadrille. Bespoke fitted costumes representing your own particular quadrille will, of course, be provided to you.

We trust you look forward to participating in this extravaganza, a housewarming Ball of the Century in honor of the new home of Mr. and Mrs. W. K. Vanderbilt at 660 Fifth Avenue in New York City.

At this, Mamma falls limply into the nearest available chair while Em shrieks for joy. *"Gosh! Oh, gosh-oh-golly!"* Em flings these shocking words about with impunity, and today, Mamma doesn't even notice.

"I guess you'll find yourself a rich husband *now!*" Em can't help gushing the words. She sounds very sure of herself and very happy for *me*, for once.

Suddenly, I can't help smiling—with relief and ... something else, something new, strange, and very welcomed: it's *joy*, so undeniable, foolish, and *fun*.

It feels absolutely marvelous.

Mamma and I look at each other wordlessly. Our eyes telegraph a message: "Em is *right*."

Suddenly … I am sick to *death* of all things Roosevelt.

There *is* a life after Roosevelt. I *know* there is, and I'm going to find it. It's not too late for me after all. Soon I'll be meeting all kinds of eligible young men—cultured, handsome, and educated men.

Rich men. Very, very rich men.

Suddenly, I realize how hard it's been on me to carry around so much weariness, always yearning and pining—wondering what Theo and Alice might be doing at any given moment, living without a man of my own, a child of my own, a *life* of my own.

I'm so unutterably *sick* of it. I'm not going to stand it anymore.

"Where's your best stationery, Mamma? I've got to answer this right away!"

The resolute glee in my voice and new stars in my eyes leave my family with *no* doubt about my answer to Mrs. Willie K. Vanderbilt.

Tonight, even after scribbling this journal entry in bed, I still can't help thinking about it ... my new life.

Yes, there *is* a new life waiting for me, I just *know* it. Somewhere out there with *some* one ... and this is my ticket out of sameness. It's my ticket up to higher ground, where happiness and fulfillment await me to claim them as my own.

Tuesday

7 February 1883

Who could possibly have "recommended" me to the stellar Alva Vanderbilt? As a "gentlewoman in reduced circumstances," I certainly don't move in the same circles as the super-rich Vanderbilts, Schemmerhorns, Astors, and Rutherfurds. (I barely move in the slightly lower circle that includes the comfortably well-off Roosevelts.)

But Aunt Annie Gracie does.

Dear, *dear* Aunt Annie, Miss Mittie's elegant, darling younger sister, has been so good to me as she tries to pull me out of my reclusive misery. She's the only person I can think of who moves easily in all sorts of social circles. I must ask her about it … when the time is right.

I'm so glad now for all of those schoolgirl dance lessons at Mr. Dodsworth's. We certainly did a lot of quadrilles back then—thank goodness!

(I experience a sudden vision of Theo's exuberant but skillful hopping dance steps; with a savage scoff, I mentally shove such thoughts away.)

I always enjoyed the stylized steps of the classical quadrille, a dance performed with four couples in a rectangular formation. Now I shall do so for an audience of *twelve hundred people* … all of them rich and well connected.

I'm on my way now, I just *know* it … I'm definitely on my way.

Friday

16 February 1883

My heart beats like a trip-hammer as I ring the bell today at the imposing front door at 660 Fifth Avenue. It's my first practice today of the Star Quadrille, right here in the same palatial mansion where it will all take place—and we're seeing it before anyone else will (except for family and servants, of course).

From what little I see of it, the glittering mansion is everything I thought it would be … *should* be: opulent, excessive, shocking, awe-inspiring, and endlessly fascinating.

The pear-shaped dancing master, Mister Edward, separates us into the designated quadrille groups: Hobby-Horse, Opera Bouffe, Mother Goose, the Star, Dresden, and Go-As-You-Please (We don't see Mrs. Vanderbilt yet; she is "out for the day.")

It's no matter. We three young "selected" ladies and four "selected" young gentlemen of the Star Quadrille start laughing and chatting as if we've been old friends for years. The fourth young lady isn't present just yet; apparently, they are holding this spot for her because she is Carrie Astor herself, daughter of the one and only queen of high society, Mrs. Astor.

Our many understudies smile less widely and more hesitantly; they keep to themselves from the sidelines. They know it's highly unlikely they'll be called upon to dance, although Mrs. Vanderbilt graciously allowed them to attend the ball in any case.

I never knew how much *fun* dancing an old-fashioned quadrille could be, especially when my partner is a suave, black-haired, young man named Henry with a fine sense of rhythm. The other dashing young men in the quadrangle are John, Joseph, and Edwin.

I'm thrilled to learn that, together, Henry and I will serve as the head couple of the Star Quadrille—definitely an honor, even ahead of Carrie Astor! The head couple performs each dance step first, and then the remaining three couples repeat the steps after we've finished. The head couple, though, always performs the steps with far more dash and style—that's part of the fun of being in this elevated position.

My heart is threatening to come right out of the top of my head, I'm so thrilled by it all...

MONDAY

19 FEBRUARY 1883

Today, we get to watch *all* of the quadrille groups perform *in costume,* and the Hobby-Horse quadrille is first on the schedule.

I have to say ... they're shockingly good! We of the Star will have to mind our Ps, Qs, and dance steps to equal (or even hope to exceed) their verve and skill.

The Hobby-Horse and the Star groups will *easily* be the best and most exciting—the Hobby-Horse maybe even more than ours because their four dancing couples are each rigged with a stuffed satin "hobby-horse." However, on the night of the party, they'll use balsa-wood horses covered by real horsehair—actual skins, manes, and tails of once-living horses! I don't know what to think of that—rather revolting, even shocking. With those cumbersome devices, *they will dance up and down the elaborate grand staircase.* It will be visually thrilling in every way! (And possibly dangerous, too.)

The other quadrilles—Dresden, Opera Bouffe, Mother Goose, and Go-As-You-Please—seem, in my opinion, more commonplace or just plain strange. (But who am I to say? It's all up to Mr. Edward.)

Then it's our turn, we of the Star Quadrille. There's an audible gasp when we four couples take the stage (and our famous performing partner, Carrie Astor, smiling ear to ear with the rest of us.) We girls each wear a different color: yellow, blue, mauve (that's me!), and white.

But that's not the stunner … it's the tiny *electric light,* nestled against a satin star, that we each wear, glued to the center of our foreheads. (For the girls, wires connected to a thumb-sized device called a "battery" have been artfully pinned inside our masses of hair. The young men dance partners hide their wires under velvet caps.)

We're also covered with sequins and satin stars on discreet wires (again protruding from our hair and our backs) like alluring fairy flowers. Our dance partners are dressed in colors to match our own. With the tiny, electric lights hanging between their eyes, they look like lascivious elves—like something out of *A Midsummer Night's Dream.* None of us has ever seen anything like this spectacle! We're dazzled with delight, shivering and shimmering with the excitement of it all.

My mauve satin slippers are accented by long, mauve-colored ribbons, crossed and recrossed over my white hose, all the way to my knees. The skirts of the dress are cunningly slit to show a shocking "length of limb."

I can't *wait* until the actual night of the performance … when, under golden illumination, our group will dazzle more than twelve hundred people with our sprite-like moves while stars glow on our foreheads.

Wednesday
21 February 1883

Three rehearsals down—three more to go.

We all have such a *grand* time together on this project—I haven't had so much fun since Theo… well … since Theo.

It was so hard to come home after each stimulating time and see Papa. He looks much more drained than usual and vastly unhappy. He speaks very little, and when he does, he seems barely coherent anymore.

Still, the hansom cab carries him off to work each morning and home again each night at 6 p.m.

Still, his brothers keep the modest stipend coming. Surely he can't go on like this much longer? Surely, something will have to … happen?

But what could it possibly be? I can see no happy ending for Papa's story—not that I ever did.

Thursday

22 February 1883

My dance partner, Henry, invited me to lunch at Delmonico's this weekend. What a spree of laughter and desserts we shall have! What did I tell you? I must be on my way … at last.

I can't wait to meet Mrs. Vanderbilt herself in person, but that will have to wait for the last dress rehearsal on 21 March, just five days before the ball. Alva Vanderbilt is said to be homely but bold and clever, an iconoclast and an innovator who refuses to take no for an answer (to anything).

Although I've not met her yet, already I admire her gumption. In less than three months, she aims to "de-throne" the reigning queen of New York society, Mrs. Caroline Schermerhorn Astor.

The aging Mrs. Astor and the self-appointed "society expert" Ward McAllister have been the arbiters of high society for as long as I can remember. They were the ones who decided if your last name was old and rich enough, or your blood blue enough, for entry into the upper echelons of society.

But things are changing and fast.

After the Civil War, and with the rise of factories and manufacturing, the number of multi-millionaires in New York City has grown like a swarm of mosquitoes over a mill pond.

Lately, Mrs. Astor and Ward McAllister have been having, as they say, "a Dickens of a time" deciding who among the nouveau riche is a diamond in the rough and who a mere pebble. This knotty problem led to the creation, a few years back, of what "they" call the Four Hundred, a select crowd of the very best people in all of New York. (The Carows got in at the tail end of this list by virtue of our prosperous, blue-blooded Kermit uncles, as well as Grandfather Tyler's faultless breeding and bloodline.)

However, there was one prominent family who desperately "wanted in" and was resolutely kept out—the Vanderbilts. Everyone knew they were crass and crude. There was no discussion—end of story.

Perhaps I Will

Then, a Vanderbilt grandson named Willie married a fiercely ambitious young woman named Alva Erksine Smith. (No, I don't know these people personally—what I *do* know comes straight from the pages of newspapers or servants' gossip gleaned by Mame.)

Above all else, Alva wanted the Vanderbilts to be accepted by the famous four hundred. She was willing to do *anything* to help effect this change, starting with commissioning the building of a fabulous new mansion at 660 Fifth Avenue at the corner of 52nd Street—the very "palace" in which I'm practicing the Star Quadrille.

Then Alva laid her plans…

Like all rich, well-connected, young women in the city, Mrs. Astor's daughter, Carrie, was waiting for her invitation to The Ball of the Century. There was even "talk" of her performing in one of the dance presentations. But when all of her wealthy friends got their invitations, hers never came: "Mother, *help*!"

Even Carrie's mother, Mrs. Astor (the reigning queen of society herself), was stumped. Her hands were tied, due to an arcane social custom regarding, of all things, calling cards (for Heaven's sake!)

Alva Vanderbilt proclaimed to all who would listen that, in all righteousness, she was precluded from inviting Carrie Astor to her extravaganza because Mrs. Astor had "never formally called upon the Vanderbilt home before."

There was only one thing Mrs. Astor could do, and she did it to please her beloved daughter. Mrs. Astor's footmen drove her out to 660 Fifth Avenue, the Vanderbilt mansion, where one of her footmen, clad in the livery of the servants of Windsor Castle in England, delivered her calling card to the maroon-clad footman of Mrs. Vanderbilt, thus formally acknowledging the latter.

The next day, the process was reversed. Alva made the trip down Fifth Avenue to have *her* card presented by *her* footman to Mrs. Astor.

In the end, Alva won the day. Correct social etiquette had been maintained, above all else, and the Vanderbilts were now accepted into the ranks of the most high.

Carrie Astor received her invitation the very next day—*plus* an invitation to dance in the Star Quadrille—and Alva Vanderbilt smugly accepted an unofficial new position as co-queen of New York society.

Thursday

8 March 1883

Miss Alva is now courting the press! With her access to endless rivers of money, she is using every available resource—including the power of the press—by inviting journalists to come in and preview the decorations before the ball begins.

Frankly enchanted newspapermen are now writing enthusiastic articles that build more excitement around the event. Just wait and see … it's going to be bigger than any ball, anywhere in the world—anytime, anywhere, by anyone ever before.

Just the other day, reporters from both the *New York Times* and the *World Herald* interviewed the eight of us dancing the Star Quadrille; we happened to be rehearsing in full costume, no less, and we looked stunning, if I do say so myself! They asked us all *sorts* of questions, mostly silly ones, like "What if you trip? What if you faint? What if you fall? And what have they been feeding you here during rehearsals?"

As Miss Alva says, it *is* going to be The Ball of the Century. And mere little *me* is going to be in the thick of it!

Friday

9 March 1883

Conie wrote me that Alice recently underwent a successful "female operation." Apparently, she can finally conceive a child now. I'm sure Theo is thrilled to the skies by the news. Speaking of news, Conie finally divulged her own momentous news: she herself is with

Perhaps I Will

child— already eight months along. *All this time* ... and she never mentioned it in her letters to me! She must be quietly mortified to have this physical evidence of her intimate physical relations with a man she doesn't love.

Only seventeen days—and nights—until the dance!

Saturday

10 March 1883

My blood runs cold. I cannot shake an ominous sense of foreboding.

It started when our front doorbell chimed early this afternoon, signaling a telegram from Western Union. (No, we still don't have a telephone. I know we have to fit it into the budget soon, somehow.) Because working hours at Kermit & Carow Ltd. also include an 8 a.m. to 3 p.m. shift on Saturdays, after an early breakfast at home of bourbon and crackers, poor Papa took a hansom cab to his office, as always.

No doubt he attempted to perform whatever kind of "work" he habitually does there (probably reading several newspapers, which makes me so heartbroken just to think of such sadness and debasement in his life). Then, per the telegram, Papa tripped and fell down a long flight of stairs, all the way from the second floor. The telegram says to come immediately because Charles Carow is, indeed, in serious condition.

I run two doors down to a friendly (and, more important, discreet) neighbor and ask to use their telephone due to a family emergency. I call our old reliable doctors Porter and Caldwell—respected, estimable, and also discreet—who have long been familiar with Papa's problems.

I beg them to come to our house as soon as possible.

Then I call Papa's office, Kermit & Carow Ltd., and speak with the office manager on duty. No one else "of consequence" is in the office today. In a voice that only quavers slightly, I speak to the manager and ask if he and another assistant might be willing to accompany my injured father home in a hansom cab. I assure him, "I'm paying all expenses for this, of course, and will gladly pay extra for your time and troubles to assist in this matter." He agrees.

After what seems like forever, Papa is carried in, flat out and feet first, through the front door by two men I don't know. Their faces reflect distant pity. I ask them to please carry him upstairs to his bedroom before the doctors arrive.

Papa's head is scraped and bloodied. He is unconscious, and his clothes are marked with grit and disheveled from his fall on the stairs. He looks like a very old vagrant—sad, shrunken, unshaven. He is fifty-eight years old.

The doctors arrive soon after; they stay by his bedside for a very long time.

Eventually, they come downstairs to talk with us, after sending Mame upstairs to sit beside him. "We hope he'll regain consciousness later today, perhaps tomorrow. Although he appears to have difficulty breathing, he seems to be stabilized. We've done everything we can for now, but we'll come by tomorrow morning to check on him."

What more can I say? Now we watch, pray, (and pay) and wait.

Tuesday

13 March 1883

Early this morning, I send out our cook's nephew—a reedy lad of about fourteen—on the run to deliver two messages. One is to dear Aunt Annie Gracie: "So very sorry, Dear Aunt, I will be unable to attend lunch at your home today with Mr. Henry Abbott. My father is very ill, and I must tend to his needs." A similar message is dispatched to Henry, my Star Quadrille dance partner, who is also invited to the same lunch (he is my "gentleman caller").

Papa finally regained consciousness—a little, for a while. But he said very little, just muttered syllables that made no sense.

Each day, he sinks more and more back into unconsciousness. His breathing remains painfully labored. Poor Papa. I shrink with pity and sadness just to listen to him.

Another rehearsal for the Star Quadrille comes and goes—without me. I am no longer part of the excitement. I also send a note, regarding my father's delicate condition and my indeterminate status as a quadrille dancer, to Mr. Edward, the dance master.

I envision Susan Hartley, the more outgoing of the female understudies for the Star Quadrille dance group, taking my place with secret pleasure.

I hope ... *hope* ... that I can soon regain my place as part of the head couple in the Star Quadrille at Mrs. Vanderbilt's Ball of the Century.

I feel ashamed and guilty for even *thinking* of something so frivolous and shallow at a time like this, as Papa hovers between life and death, but I can't help thinking it. Just when my life has finally become so rich and full with enticing possibilities ...

Thursday

15 March 1883

I see that the "great" socialist/philosopher (great in his own mind, at least) Karl Marx died yesterday. He was sixty-four.

Papa is no better today. He is fifty-eight.

Friday

16 March 183

Papa breathes with even greater difficulty—unevenly and heavily. *Stentorian*, I believe the proper word is.

His skin is so waxy, he no longer looks real, just a shrunken vestige of his former elegant, kind-hearted, and drink-and-drug-addicted self.

Here we are, all of us, Mamma, Em, Mame, the cook, and Brooks, the housemaid—and me. We are all "paused" in the midst of life, wondering what will become of us all if anything should happen to Papa.

Perhaps I Will

I know it's horrible and selfish of me, but—I don't want dear Papa to ever wake up. Life has mostly been utter *misery* for him. Just one long, joyless, drawn-out, drained-out ebbing of life, I'm thinking—except, of course, for our lovely trips to the theater together and our times, sitting in wordless companionship, listening to the whippoorwill on the windowsill…

SATURDAY

17 MARCH 1883

Today, the air rings with raucous Irish joy. It's St. Patrick's Day, the day the Irish parade up and down the streets … and the day that my dearest Papa breathed his last, with his family and doctors at his side.

It was all very quiet. I felt only a great hollowness within, an anti-climax. I will always remember how brightly the sun shone this morning.

After seven days of pain and struggles to breathe, Papa is beyond it all now. There were no deathbed words or longing looks. Papa never regained consciousness, and he died in his "sleep."

Obdurately, I make myself remember only the *good* times with Papa ... how he encouraged my love of fairy tales, books, and especially the theater and how he coached me in Latin, bird-watching, and plant identification. Mostly, I think of how he encouraged my interest in the wonderful wide world out there (which makes me think of the Star Quadrille, prompting weak tears to slide down my cheeks).

On the death certificate, the doctors write that he died of pericarditis (inflammation of the heart muscle), pneumonia, and something they call "asthenia" (general weakness)—as the doctors explain to me with low-voiced bluntness: "In other words, the sickness of a habitual drinker."

This afternoon, with help from Mamma and Em, I write up a very brief death announcement—not a true obituary, just a notice—to run the following day in the *Times*, listing details about the brief funeral we're planning for Papa. At the bottom, at Mamma's request, I include the phrase, "Please omit flowers."

With this completed, I write two notes on Mamma's best stationery—one to Mr. Edward, the dance master, and another to Mrs. Willie Vanderbilt herself—offering my "deep and sincere regret that I must withdraw from dancing in the Star Quadrille because of the death of my father this morning."

I make sure that our cook's nephew—our busy messenger boy—is properly (soberly) dressed. I slip a black armband over his left sleeve before he rushes off to deliver these messages. I prepay him with a bonus cash amount, along with serious admonitions for him to "hurry yet be careful, and make *sure* each message gets to its intended recipient."

Poor Papa, bless him always. At least he's removed from his misery of a life. I am now removed, too. I'm removed from life, expected to wear black "mourning weeds" for a full year.

Destiny or providence chastened me for trying to get ahead of myself. It pulled me back from reaching out to any help or any hope (except sheer coincidence or happenstance) of a new, full life.

JUST BEFORE BEDTIME

TUESDAY

20 MARCH 1883

It was a very quiet, midday funeral.

St. Mark's Church in the Bowery of Greenwich Village looked—now, as always—somehow reassuring to me. The double columns, old-fashioned portico, and clean, classic steeple … never changing throughout turbulent years.

Unlike myself.

The Kermit & Carow Ltd. brothers showed up, but very few others attended.

Perhaps I Will

Hugely pregnant now, Conie Roosevelt Robinson didn't attend. It simply isn't done. Besides, she lives so far away now, someplace called Orange, New Jersey.

Theodore wasn't there, either. He's still hard at work in Albany with the Legislature. Even Miss Mittie (visiting family in Georgia), Bamie Roosevelt (on a lengthy visit to distant cousins), Fanny Smith Dana (off with her new husband on military business), and most of the girls from my school didn't attend. One beloved Roosevelt representative *did* show up: Aunt Annie Gracie. She brought with her a surprising companion—Alice Lee Roosevelt (who, I am sure, only attended as a favor to Aunt Annie). The words of the Episcopal service washed over me … "We have come here today to remember before God our brother, Charles Carow, and to give thanks for his life, to commend him to God, our merciful redeemer and judge, to commit his body to be buried, and to comfort one another in our grief"…I experience a literal spasm—a death of something—inside me, and then, suddenly, in its place, I felt the cleanliness of … peace.

My inner cankerworm of jealousy–always that jealousy of Alice—was finally dead.

After the service, as funeral attendees offered final condolences and bid us goodbye under the church's portico, I found myself standing in front of Aunt Annie—and Alice.

Alice looked fetching, as always—even in black. Vague rumors about town continue to whisper that young Mrs. Roosevelt *may* now finally be pregnant. All I felt was a resigned—yet oddly comforting—feeling that everything had finally "come right."

I knew things were as they should be: Theo and Alice, happily ever after together, world without end, amen.

After I thank and hug Aunt Annie, I turn to Alice (who looks a bit askance at the prospect that I might actually try to hug her … no, I'm not going to go *that* far…)

But suddenly I'm clutching Alice's gloved right hand in both of mine. I whisper, over

Perhaps I Will

and over, hardly knowing what I say: "Thank you ... oh, thank you ... it was *so* kind of you to come..."

Still clutching Alice's hand, I start bending over to one side, like the bird with a broken wing again.

My whispers suddenly become audible, ugly, gulping, gasping sobs.

Not like my stand-offish, reserved self at *all*.

Although I am absolutely mortified, I cannot seem to stop: "Thank you, Alice ... oh, thank you ... I'm *so* very sorry ... *so* sorry..."

Mercifully, Aunt Annie finally extricates Alice from my clutches. Shooting me a look of pity laced with mercy, Aunt Annie links her arm through Alice's, and they are gone.

Papa will be buried later this week—so appropriate on this holy week of Easter. Not far from his final resting place is the glittering locale people call "The Ladies' Mile," a strip of fashionable shops with big windows full of spring fashions.

I, however, will be wearing black for many months—probably years—to come.

Papa's death occurs only days before what could have been ... should have been ... the most brilliant social event of my entire life.

Somehow, though, I don't feel bitter, nor am I trembling with rage.

Destiny is obviously telling me something: know your place and make your peace with it. You have been born to do good works for others. If it were not so, your life would be different. It's not. It is the same. It will *always* be the same. Get used to it and accept it.

World without end, amen.

Follow Edie's saga as it continues in Book 3,
World Without End, Amen

A new world and another chance?

While Edie still tries to make a life for herself, sudden tragedy strikes without warning: so earth-shattering that it changes everything and everyone in her world.

Taking stock of her life, Edie realizes that fate has left nothing—and no one—for her in New York City. It's time to make a new start someplace else.

When she overhears talk about a far-off paradise where an American can live an inexpensive yet still luxurious life, Edie knows that *this* is the next best step for the hapless, hopeless Carow women.

Determined to make the best of their collective lives—and perhaps remake herself into the artist she often dreamed of becoming—Edie sets out to cross the Atlantic and leave behind all things Roosevelt.

Will Edie make a brand new life? Or will destiny come calling, yet again, with an even stranger set of circumstances than before?

Take a sneak peek into Chapter One of *World Without End, Amen*

Copyright © 2021 by Jane Susann MacCarter

Publishing Services provided by Paper Raven Books
Printed in the United States of America
First Printing, 2021

Jane Susann MacCarter
World Without End, Amen
Edie in Love Series
Book Three

Hardcover ISBN= 978-1-7368789-4-1
Paperback ISBN= 978-1-7368789-5-8

Subjects: Edith Kermit Carow, Theodore Roosevelt II, Alice Hathaway Lee, United States First Lady, 26th President of United States, Gilded Age, Victorian romance, 1880s politics, coming-of-age

*To my dear son, Kent Edward MacCarter,
also my cheerleader and steadfast publisher of
deserving poets.*

World Without End, Amen

How well I remember—dear God, do I ever remember!—how dark my days grew after Papa's death. There was nothing to be done about it, just more resignation on my part, more endurance, and more pasting-on of placid smiles so that no one sees my pain—something impoverished gentlewomen know all too well.

Because of a quirk of destiny, my one chance for new happiness—as a featured dancer at Mrs. Vanderbilt's lavish Ball of the Century—passed me by in the blink of an eye.

One day, I was "in"—then suddenly, I was "out." I never even saw it coming, or leaving.

What are those words again from the New Testament? Something about "Whoever has 'not,' even his Nothing shall be taken away." (Or, in my case, her Nothing is taken away...)

Yes, my Nothing is now well and truly "away" ... trampled, lifeless, and kicked to the corner. What's even the point of going on?

What's it all for?

Friday

23 March 1883

Papa is being buried today. On Good Friday—so fitting.

The gloomy weather matches our sense of loss, hollowness, and inevitable change.

Of the many qualities that may be attributed to Charles Carow in this earthly life—marked by misfortune, falling short, becoming weak, or helplessly shallow—let it also be said that, in many small ways, he was an angel.

At least to *me*.

Sunday

25 March 1883

It's Easter Sunday today.

I can only imagine the hurricane of activity rampaging through the home of Willie and Alva Vanderbilt today. Tomorrow night is the Ball of the Century.

World Without End, Amen

I must buy *all* of the newspapers the next morning—not just the staid old *Times*—to learn all about it.

I must—

Enough.

Very late Monday Night
26 March 1883

Tonight is the momentous Ball of the Century.

I'm still awake and watching the clock, imagining what's happening moment by moment.

It's 10 p.m. Carriages will line the driveway to deposit gaily dressed guests at the Vanderbilt's front door. Mobs of gawkers will press in on all sides. The police will hold them back.

Miss Alva will be there in the grand reception room, receiving her twelve hundred guests—she couldn't *possibly* press that many hands in greeting, could she?

On the dot of half past eleven, I know that the Hobby-Horse Quadrille group begins to "gallopade" (as Miss Alva likes to say) up and down the grand staircase in complex dance steps.

After the Hobby-Horse group comes the fairy-tale creatures from Mother Goose and then the Opera Bouffe ... after which it's time for ... the Star.

We of the Star Quadrille ... but I am not part of a "we" any longer.

That gloating understudy, Susan Hartley—wearing *my* fantastical, impossibly beautiful costume with the tiny, electric light glowing on her forehead—will captivate the crowds with her fellow dancers as they dip, sway, and sashay.

After the Dresden and Go-As-You-Please sets, the dancers will part in a shower of shimmering, tinsel stars ... stepping back to reveal Miss Alva herself, who will announce in a voice that carries beautifully across the enormous room, "I now pronounce the Ball of the Century *open* ... to all dancers!"

I won't sleep at all tonight.

LATER:
I didn't sleep, at all.

World Without End, Amen

I want to read about it in the papers before they're all sold out.

Tuesday

27 March 1883

Shortly after dawn today (around 6:45 a.m.)—still wide awake from the night before—I leave the house quietly. Mamma and Em are still snoring away as I head out to purchase the early papers.

First, instead of heading for a newsstand, somehow I "find myself" (I'm ashamed to say) walking along Fifth Avenue inexorably toward Miss Alva's house. Just to … to…

Just to still be part of it, somehow.

I'm glad I do because the streets are literally streaming with fantastical characters from another world. Costumed party-goers are still spilling out of the imposing front doors of the Vanderbilt mansion.

That's right … I remember now Miss Alva's schedule. The party was scheduled to conclude promptly at 6 a.m. after a farewell Virginia reel.

Hundreds of inebriated party guests now stumble about in the early light of day, waiting for carriages with liveried servants to pick them up or calling out for one of the scores of hansom cabs parked along the road. Yes, the police are still very much in evidence—everywhere—to "keep the peace."

Many children (beginning their morning walks to school), together with troops of newspaper reporters (following up on last night's big story), mingle with and smile at the noisy, laughing guests.

I watch for a while, but then it starts making me feel queasy. I leave in search of the morning papers.

Back at home, only Cook and the housemaid are up, so I'm left to myself at the dining room table. A comforting cup of English breakfast tea is safely encircled by my right hand; heaps of newspapers are splayed out before me on the table.

With perverse pleasure and gnawing pain, I start to read the coverage—page, after page, after page—about the Ball of the Century. I don't want to miss even one tiny nugget of news.

"Crowds of onlookers, restrained with difficulty by scores of policemen, pressed forward to catch glimpses of debutantes and members of New York society, attired in their fancy dress costumes, as they were escorted into the mansion."

The papers say that many party guests came dressed as Louis XVI—safety in numbers, I guess. Also glimpsed were King Lear ("but one in his right mind, hopefully"), Joan of Arc, Daniel Boone, Queen Elizabeth I, and even Father Knickerbocker.

Society's Arbiter Ward McAllister was also there, resplendent in purple velvet and scarlet silk (it didn't say who his character was), while Mrs. Chauncey Depew was a vision in "sea-green satin with clusters of silk water lilies" (not sure who she represented, either).

Hundreds of other guests came as pirates, princesses, peacocks, eagles, medieval peasants, and menacing highwaymen ... and two ladies even came as "creatures"—one a hornet and the other a cat. (Apparently. the latter even sewed stuffed cat heads onto her dress—ugh.)

While Miss Alva looked queenly as a "bejeweled Venetian Renaissance princess," her very own sister-in-law, Alice Claypoole Gwynn, upstaged Miss Alva—and *everybody* else—by showing up as "The Electric Light." (What *is* it about Alices anyway? Always managing to be the most breathtaking woman in a room.) Alice Gwynn's stunning gown, made of white satin and trimmed with diamonds and small electric light bulbs, was devised around several of hidden "battery" devices; she literally "lit up the room" as only an electric light bulb can.

Of course, electricity is all the rage now, so I'm not surprised someone capitalized on the idea, especially when a couple of New York streets are already illuminated by this marvel—with many more to come. Thomas Edison's generating station on Pearl Street actively seeks more business.

I read on, and on:

"Twelve hundred gaily costumed figures danced and drank amid the flower-filled house, including the third-floor gymnasium that was converted into a forest filled with palm trees and draped with bougainvillea and orchids. Dinner was served at 2 a.m. by the chefs of Delmonico's, working together with the Vanderbilt's platoons of servants. The dancing continued until the sun was rising. Diamonds and other jewels glinted in the changing light. Mrs. Vanderbilt led her guests in one final Virginia reel, and, with that, the ball was over."

I see that the *Times* even printed the names of all the quadrille dancers—they have to, of course, because we are no "mere dancers per se," but each of us a member of New York society (to varying degrees) in our own right. Yes … here I am, listed on page three: "Miss Edith Kermit Carow," one of the Star Quadrille dancers.

This will make Miss Understudy Hartley simply furious. But of course the name lists of everyone and everything were all supplied to the press far in advance.

I'm sure no one who counted ever realized I was among the missing.

A small voice inside my head chides me: *Remember, you're not the only one. Theo is among "the missing," too.*

All of the Roosevelts were "missing" for the Ball of the Century. Theo and Alice were too far away and too occupied with legislative matters and Albany society to attend. Hugely pregnant Conie understandably could not be seen in society. Elliott was out of the continent again—Europe, or maybe India—I can't remember which. Bamie and Miss Mittie were both under the weather (a frequent occurrence for them both), "taking the waters" at an out-of-state spa. Aunt Annie Gracie joined their journey to keep them company.

However, the Roosevelts are different. *All* of them. They don't seem to crave—or need—validation from high society. Each Roosevelt seems confident and secure in his or her own worth, just as they stand. They don't need Alva Vanderbilt to validate their existence.

Nor do I. (But still…)

Enough of this.

I will say I'm perversely pleased to see that the *New York Sun* published a *very* stern article, critiquing the Ball's "shocking excesses" when there is still so much "suffering" in this city and outside of the city, too. The Ball of the Century shared the front page of the *New York Times* with the recovery of bodies from the Diamond Coal mine disaster.

Shallow and wasteful or not, this ball is already on its way to becoming a legend of the century. A hundred years (or more) will come and go before anyone fails to remember the Ball of the Century for its over-the-top opulence, extravagance, and style.

Together with the venerable Mrs. Astor, society now has a new co-queen. Miss Alva got what she wanted, and she's already glorying in it—I just know.

No one will ever forget this night. Certainly not me.

CPSIA information can be obtained
at www.ICGtesting.com
Printed in the USA
LVHW050202100122
708115LV00012B/244